NO OTHER PLACE

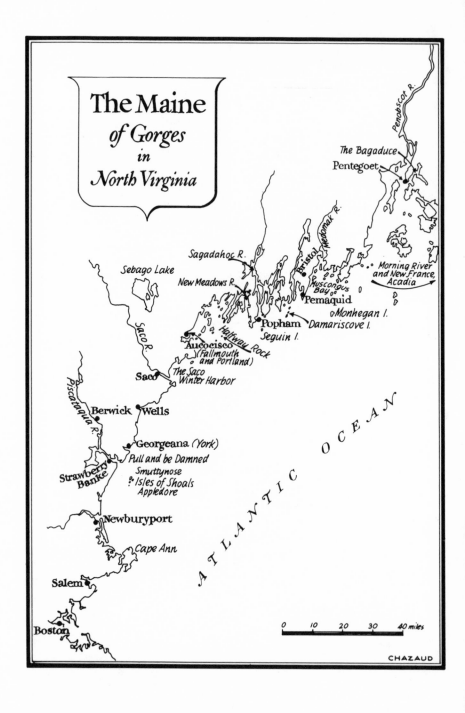

The Maine
of Gorges
in
North Virginia

Penobscot R.

The Bagaduce
Pentegoet

Sagadahoc R.

Sebago Lake

New Meadows R.

Bristol

Medomak R.

Morning River
and New France,
Acadia

Muscongus
Bay

Pemaquid

Monhegan I.

Popham

Damariscove I.

Seguin I.

Halfway Rock

Saco R.

Aucocisco
(Fallmouth
and Portland)

Saco

The Saco
Winter Harbor

Piscataqua R.

Berwick

Wells

Georgeana (York)

Pull and be Damned

Strawberry
Banke

Smuttynose
Isles of Shoals
Appledore

Newburyport

Cape Ann

ATLANTIC OCEAN

Salem

Boston

0   10   20   30   40 miles

CHAZAUD

No Other Place

John Gould

W · W · Norton & Company

New York   London

The text of this book is composed in Janson, with display type set in
Goudy Bold. Composition and manufacturing by The Maple-Vail Book
Manufacturing Group. Book design by Holly McNeeley.

First Edition

Library of Congress Cataloging in Publication Data

Gould, John, 1908–
No other place.

I. Title.
PS3513.Ô852N6 1984   813'.52   83–23710

ISBN 0-393-01850-4

W. W. Norton & Company, Inc.
500 Fifth Avenue, New York, N. Y. 10110
W. W. Norton & Company Ltd.
37 Great Russell Street, London WC1B 3NU

1 2 3 4 5 6 7 8 9 0

FOR EMERSON MORSE BULLARD

This was all quite a good bit
before my time.

(Signed) Peter Partout
Peppermint Corner

Warning:

Every school child knows that Saint Augustine was settled in 1565, and is our oldest community. Of course, Jacques Cartier was doing business at Tadoussac on the Saint Lawrence River in 1534, and Tadoussac seems to have been sixty-six years old before the historians permitted it to be settled in 1600. Curious, is it not? Consider, then, the visit to Maine in 1556 of André Thêvet. He wrote that he found people living on Monhegan Island, where, in fact, Europeans had been living for something like 400 years. Thêvet was amused that some Indians appeared, eager to trade, and that they were dressed in European-made clothes. Further, they were rowing a fairly large round-bottom boat of a style common in Britanny. This book is not meant to be primarily historical, but the reader need not presume an error if he finds herein some history not yet taught in school.

1

Helpful suggestions:

The Huguenot name Quintaille, encountered in Chapter 2, should be read with an approximate French pronunciation. Thus: *can-tigh-y'h*. The French liquid *l*.

Jules should be rendered as *zheel*, the *e* sound of *u* or the *u* sound of *e*, depending on who was your first French teacher.

"Down East" should be taken as a direction rather than a place. In Casco Bay, Pemaquid is down east, and at Pemaquid, Castine is down east. At Pemaquid, Eastport is far down east, and Machias would be pretty far down. To Mainers, Nova Scotians and New Brunswickers are down easters. Down East is a never-never land.

And once again—The Maine was "down wind" from Boston. One sailed down to Maine, or down east. Then a boat would beat back up wind to return to Boston. So you always go down to Maine and up to Boston. There is no other way.

NO OTHER PLACE

1

How did the settlers on the American prairies decide where to put their homes? There they were, about to set up in business, and the land was flat and straight forever. Why was one place taken instead of another? Why not twenty feet this way? Or that way? What difference? But when Jabez Knight built his house at Morning River, in that part of North America known as North Virginia, which happens today to be the State of Maine, he had no such decision to make. There was only the one spot for his house—the sunrise side of the hill by the second cataract, where the wide meadow of Morning River begins. Five hundred acres were in that meadow, more or less, and when it was surveyed a lifetime later, it was more. Jabez's front door opened on the Atlantic Ocean, off over the lower cataract, the tidal estuary of Morning River, and—as he said—on Spain. There was no other place.

Jabez found Morning River in a fog. It was summertime; the year was 1611. In his sailing dory he had been scouting for boat lumber, and somewhere east of the

Penobscot River he beached out for the night and woke the next morning in a thick mull. He stayed there two days, and in the distance could hear running water. The morning the fog scaled off he sailed into the inland cove across the gut and found the waterfalls he had heard. They were at the end of tidewater, well up the gooseneck cove. Stepping ashore, he found the ancient Redman's footpath from the lower falls up over the rise, and came to the second falls. They were not, the two cataracts, a hundred yards apart, but between them the river, he learned later, made a deadwater sweep around the meadowland. Three hundred years later, Professor Parker Cleaveland, the geologist at Bowdoin College, would bring his students here to see this whimsy of the glaciers. The river should have gone directly from the upper falls to the lower, making one long raceway, but the glacier had piled up debris, the valley filled with water, and for centuries silt came down to settle and level off the meadowland. When pressure broke through, a channel meandered to encompass the built-up silt.

Looking as he was for boat stock, it happened to be juniper, Jabez merely admired the situation on that morning and moved along. It was a beautiful place; one to be remembered. He moved along.

There is, and there was then, a village on the west shore of the Medomak River, at Muscongus Bay, named Bristol. In 1607 the English had tried to settle at Popham Beach, on the Sagadahock River, but a year later the folks gave up. Most returned to England, but a few moved over around Pemaquid Point and up Muscongus Bay to build some cabins and try anew. This handful was from Bristol in England, so the name of their American town is accounted for. They made a wise move, as Popham Beach was hardly meant at the Creation to nurture pioneers. Wild cucumbers, beach roses, bayberries, sand, surf, exposure, and desolation. But around Pemaquid Point and up Muscongus Bay, seafood was plentiful, game was handy, the soil was agreeable, and the cabins were sheltered from the open sea. Ten miles down the bay, Monhegan Island stood as the landfall of North America—a rendezvous for European vessels and a market for cured fish and hides.

Sixteen years old, Jabez Knight came to Bristol in 1610, apprentice to Warren Quintaille, master boatwright and joiner, a Huguenot who, after a few years in England, foresaw prosperity for his trade in a new land of codfish. Jabez stayed with Warren Quintaille two years, but was indentured for seven. During those two years he and Warren built eight sloops together and alone Jabez had made himself his pride and joy—the sailing dory in which he had gone to the east'ard looking for junipers. It was when he returned from that expedition to Bristol that, by request, he terminated his apprenticeship.

Earlier that year he had been in the bow of a sloop, fitting the "ceiling," and Warren Quintaille's dark-eyed daughter Elzade came crawling in to see how the work was coming along. Elzade had done this when she was fourteen, and when she was fifteen, but now Elzade was sixteen. She had cried hysterically afterwards, and clung a-tremble to Jabez for a long time. He held her while she sobbed, and until she looked up at him and smiled. When Mother Quintaille observed that her daughter was up a stump, Jabez was given the usual choice—get married or get going. But in truth he had not made the decision—Elzade wouldn't marry him until he could provide. "Come for me when you can," she said. So Jabez was back, had decided to call the place Morning

River, and was fitting logs for a cabin. He fitted logs, too, for a boatshop, and sailed out to Monhegan Island to tell the boys that he was in business. Nothing was done swiftly, or easily. He cobbed up a wharf. He studied the lower falls day after day, figuring out how to harness the flow for his mill. He started to clear garden space in the meadow. The second summer he went to Monhegan Island again and sent his request to the Plymouth Company in England—a deed to the quadrangle at Morning River.

Instead of a deed, he got a "bond for a deed." As soon as he completed paying the fifteen pounds, the Plymouth Company would forward a good and sufficient deed, authority of the grant and charter of James I, and in the meantime credit would be applied for hides and other commodities delivered to the company agents at Monhegan, Damariscove, Sassanoa, and Pemaquid. It was mostly from repairing boats that Jabez finally paid this debt, and it was eighteen years later. He now had his wheel and sawmill, as well as the sloop he made—the *Elzada* was not large, but large enough to bring his millstones. And, he had acquired Jules Marcoux.

Ah! Jules Marcoux! There was a type! Jules had come over the ancient "long trail," just looking the country over, and he had walked out of the woods one morning to greet Jabez with a cheerful "Bonjour!" Jabez knew no French; Jules had no English. But they teamed up, and Jules stayed at Morning River until he died. It was a strange friendship in a wild country so often to bristle with strife between French and English. Three times, his first summer, Jules had walked out toward Canada to make purchases. A yoke of young oxen, a milking cow, some hens, and tools. These would come, sooner or later, on sloops heading westerly. The cattle were hoist to the wharf by Jabez's winch, and were much relieved. They had been seasick and each sloop needed washing down after a trip. Jules learned to run the mill. He planted the garden. He cut wood. And slowly he mastered his "small" English. Jabez never learned French. And while Jabez was finishing his timbered house, Jules made another house, down by the lower falls, for himself. He took great pains with ornamental "gingerbread." The carpentry of Jabez was sturdy and useful; that of Jules was sturdy, useful, and beautiful. Jabez said, "The only thing we need now are wives."

"I want for talk to you about him," said Jules. Best he could, he made it known that he had left his Marie-Paule somewhere back by the Bay of Fundy, along with three children, and had neglected to speak of them. Jabez started, "What the hell . . ." and then realized Jules wouldn't understand him if he said more. Jules took the *Elzada* and went to fetch Marie-Paule, 'Tit Jules, Cécile, and Omar. When he brought them, Jabez gave him a paper assuring him of a life interest in Morning River Farm, and Marie-Paule took over as mistress of the establishment. Jabez, then, took the *Elzada* and went to the westward to learn what he might of Elzade.

Which was nothing. The baby would be as old now as Jabez had been when he left Bristol! Master Quintaille was all but forgotten; nobody knew anything about Elzade. Jabez was pleased to have the lines of his *Elzada* admired, and took an order for a sloop like her. He and Jules finished it the next winter, and after the garden was planted Jabez sailed off to find a bride. "I'll be gone until I come back," he said, and Marie-Paule tidied the *Elzada* and ripped off numerous do's and don't's of which Jabez understood not one word. "Bon voyage!" said Jules, and then, "Bimeby!" It took a week to bring the *Elzada*

by the wind to Strawberry Banke. There was something of a settlement there, and an inn with a good flip—
and a chance to get acquainted. Jabez stayed on the sloop,
and wandered up to the inn each afternoon for a flip
and a look-about. People who take their flip are never
all bad, and soon Jabez was introduced to Martha Blake,
who protested that she was not given to spirits as a general rule, but under the circumstances could be prevailed upon. Jabez suspected she had so decided before
he asked her.

She was a widow, Martha Townes Blake, and Jabez
was pleased that she looked not unlike Marie-Paule
Marcoux, who was extremely pretty. Her widowhood
was recent, and from the way she spoke of it the tragedy had not been all that sad. She had been brought to
America from Hull, England, as a bride, and the late
Mr. Blake had built a cabin at Sebago Lake, where he
planned to remain indefinitely. Jabez got the idea Mrs.
Blake hadn't taken to this with unbridled enthusiasm.
Then one day as they were having their frugal noon-
time meal, the door latch was lifted and an Indian walked
in to sit at table with them. This was not unusual in
those times, and the prudent pioneer offered food and
after a while the Indian would go away. Mr. Blake,
however, with a deep sense of English possession,
revealed his resentment at this intrusion, whereat the
Indian knocked him in the head. Mrs. Blake, suddenly
a widow, buried her husband, deserted the cabin, and
was on her way to ask shelter from a younger brother
in Salem when her journey had been interrupted at
Strawberry Banke. "So that's my story," she told Jabez.

On the third day following that, she went for a sail
with Jabez on the *Elzada*. "What a good name for a boat,"
she said, "I like it!" Jabez dissembled that he had heard

it somewhere or other and thought at the time it would make a fine name for a sloop. "I like it," she said again. Now, there is a tide run in the Piscataqua River, and a fast one, and there is a narrows called Pull-and-be-damned. No oarsman can make progress against the flow, and sailing craft must wait for the turn of tide. Jabez, aware of this, contrived to be downstream on an ebbing tide when it was time to return his lady to the shore.

During that night at sea, after a hearty supper and a friendly brandy in the intimacy of the *Elzada*'s comfortable cabin, Martha told Jabez that she was twenty-eight years old, that her husband had lacked either finesse or faculty, and that until now she had never truly known love. This pleased Jabez and he offered to take her on as a steady student, so in Strawberry Banke the next day he inquired about the facilities for a marriage. There was a snag.

Jabez, and the other Bristolites, had been Episcopalian. Martha had been Catholic, but her Separatist husband had eroded that and she wasn't sure now just where she stood. The combination schoolmaster and clergyman who came from Newburyport every second Sunday by horse was a sturdy old Sid. Sussex who would never want his daughter to eat a white egg, and it was doubtful if he would bless this union. Besides, why wait two weeks? Martha solved everything.

"Why the hell not?" she asked when she thought of it. So Jabez, as captain of the sloop *Elzada*, married the happy couple at sea. Jabez got Martha's effects aboard, and they sluiced down through Pull-and-be-damned on an outgoing daybreak tide. Well at sea before the morning warmed up, they had left Appledore behind and were homeward bound for Morning River. A following wind was warm and propitious. Martha came up from the cabin undressed, and Jabez took a hint. "A good sloop can sail herself," he said. The *Elzada* was a good sloop. He tied the tiller and they went below. It was the twenty-third of August, 1632. They stood there naked in the cabin, holding hands, and exchanged their vows. Jabez tried to sound ecclesiastical. "Do you take me for your lawful wedded husband?" he asked.

"You're goddamn right!"

And Jabez said, "In that case I pronounce us man and wife."

Martha was standing straight up, but Jabez lacked head room in the cabin, so he craned and was sort of closer to her than she to him. He kissed her, and a honeymoon was not significantly delayed. The *Elzada* held course on a good chance-along, and it was well after dark that Jabez pulled on some clothes and came on deck. The Great Bear was exactly where he expected it, and some time tomorrow Monhegan Island would be where it ought to be. Bride and bridegroom would be at Morning River before night fell again. Should Martha be well asleep, he called softly down into the cabin, "Everything all right?"

Her reply was on the sleepy side: "Goddamn right!"

2

A great many vessels, one kind and another over the years, have passed east and west by Morning River without seeing it. Jabez had found it by chance, thanks to fog. There are two islands, now called Long Razor and Outer Razor, that obscure the river's tidal estuary from the open ocean. Then the estuary has its gooseneck, so a vessel must be well inside before the two cascades can be seen. Jabez knew what was in store, and he knew the afternoon sun would highlight the scene. For arriving, he had on pants and shirt, and Martha was below, condescending to the formality of a dress after a warm sailing day of nothing at all. Jabez stood astride the tiller, holding it steady in his crotch as the *Elzada* came around Outer Razor Ledges. As the rudder felt the tide-run, he reached down a hand to "stiddy-off." The *Elzada* eased, and moments later would be making into the estuary. "Come up," he called—"you don't want to miss this!"

Martha, coming up, went into a spasm of hysterics. She grabbed at the cheeserind, clung to it, and whooped in uncontrolled laughter until she lost her breath. She gulped, gained control, and pointing at the tiller thrusting up from Jabez's groin, she said, "I thought you were playing with yourself!" So that first glimpse of Morning River had to wait for Martha—it would be some years before she would be at sea again.

"You gormed it, Bunny Rabbit!" said Jabez. He laid the *Elzada* smoothly to the wharf, passed a line around a spile, let the mains'l hang limp in the lee, and turned to pick up Martha and carry her ceremoniously across the threshold—*Elzada* to the wharf. "Welcome home," he said.

Martha snuggled in his arms. "I have a feeling about arriving home," she said. "It's a special feeling. I've never had it before and I'm not sure. It's a good feeling. I think I'm knocked up!"

Then, over Jabez's shoulder, she saw Jules Marcoux. Jules had come down the path at the arrival of the *Elzada* to find them embraced in a manner that promised to continue for some time. He took advantage of their distraction to look Martha over. There was definite approval on his face when Martha noticed him. "A man!" she whispered at Jabez. The man, now gaining a better view, continued to assess Martha, and while it was a close contest, he thought perhaps Marie-Paule had an advantage across the front. "I guess I didn't speak of him," said Jabez. "This is Jules Marcoux, our associate at Morning River—Jules, this is my wife, Martha."

"Ah, now," thought Jules as Martha came to him with a hand forward, "she's got good walk!" Marie-Paule was smaller in the hips and had had trouble with the babies; this woman was better, Jabez had good womans! "Enchanté!" he said, and Martha turned to Jabez. "What does *that* mean?"

Jules laughed. "Dat mean happy for make know you; happy for 'ave Madame Knight; happy for friend Jabez; happy for Marie-Paule get companies." He cocked his head as he shook her hand, and although he spoke to Martha he was looking at Jabez when he said, "Ver' pretty womans!"

"First time I saw her," Jabez said, "she made me think of Marie-Paule."

"Ah! Marie-Paule! He not know about Madame Lady Knight!" Jules hurried up the path to break the news.

"Are you really pregnant? I'd be so happy!"

"No more than me. My guess is I've been honeymooned into a permanent job. I'm up a stump higher than a kite. It's a guess, but I think I'm a good guesser."

So now Martha came to be mistress of Morning River Farm, and she and Marie-Paule shared share-and-share-alike all their lives. When Martha stepped into Jabez's big house, a memory of the dirt-floored cabin at Sebago Lake made her shudder. For what it was, it was a good pioneer home, as good as most. But this! There was nothing at Strawberry Banke so fine as this house at Morning River; she had heard that her brother had lately built a beautiful home at Salem, but it certainly would be no better than hers. Jabez had said they could go to the west'ard after a while and she could find things she needed or wanted. No need—Marie-Paule had taken care of everything. Martha learned how she did it. A vessel, coasting by, would come up the Morning River estuary, and there would be Jules and Jabez rigging the hoist to bring something ashore. Across on Outer Razor lived Manny the Portygee, and when he wasn't to the east'ard fishing the Bank, he would be to the west'ard trading. Tell Manny what you wanted, and . . .

And Morning River, remote as it was, was anything

but a lonely place. More often than Martha had expected, a sloop would come for repairs, or to buy buckets, oars, chests, and things Jules liked to make. There was one schooner that came often, a coaster from the islands passing up to the Gaspésie and Newfoundland. The crew had a huge blackamoor who played the squeezebox and sang a beautiful baritone. Jules played the fiddle. Marie-Paule had the voice of a lark, and knew all the songs of Provence. The party at the Marcoux house when this vessel paused overnight at Morning River would leave Marie-Paule hoarse for two days. This was the schooner that kept the Morning River cellars in rum and molasses, and before the blackamoor was permitted to eat, drink, play, and sing, he was obliged to show, once again, how he could nimbly, and alone, roll a cask into the cellar on a plank. At the first such party after Martha came, she and Jabez danced, but Marie-Paule made them stop with words about a *fausse-couche*. Jules protested. "Not for her, doze *fausse-couche*—bimeby, you see." Martha waited her time, and thought often that she owed her thanks to an Indian up at Sebago Lake.

The child was born on schedule, with Marie-Paule in full command, and Jules and Jabez sitting on the washstand by the back steps—looking off at the ocean. Perfectly good girl child. Jules told Marie-Paule, "You see? What I tol' you!" Martha told Jabez, "I'm going to name her for the sloop."

Jabez said, "I like that," and turned to look out the bedroom window, down the estuary, over the islands, and to sea. "I like that," he said. Elzada. Elzade. Martha knew nothing about Elzade. He, as to the sloop, was always careful to say el-zay-duh, and sometimes as he said it he thought el-zahd. Marie-Paule always called the sloop el-zahd, and now she would call baby Elzada el-zahd, too. Jabez smiled to think that Elzada would be competent in two languages before she was six. No, three—because she would have to talk with Jules Marcoux, too. He fancied Elzada saying, "Doze woman, he . . ." and "Dat h'oxen's was got some hay." Elzahd. El-zay-duh. Jabez turned from the window back to Martha. Martha would never know about Elzade. He hoped not. He took her hand. "Thank you for my daughter Elzada," he said.

3

Martha didn't know about Naddah the Micmac. Soon
after Jules Marcoux had come out of the woods to live
at Morning River Farm, Jabez heard him up by the house
greeting somebody in great joy. And he came down at
once to where Jabez was with two men—Father Bois
and Naddah the Micmac. They didn't know Jabez and
Jules were there. Father Bois was a teacher and priest
at Lac Raffine, and had been curious about the "long
trail" when Naddah told of it. The oyster beds that had
brought the Paint People over the trail for their coastal
feasts had long disappeared, and for a thousand years
no new shells had been thrown on the midden at Morning River. Naddah thought he could find the trail and
led the priest, promising him a feed of trout at the falls.
Jabez had found the tidal end of that trail on his first
coming to Morning River, where it left salt water and
went up from the lower falls to the second. He had
noticed how soft moccasins, brought by the lay of the
ground always to the same spot, had worn a hollow in
the granite. It was hard to believe in the silence and

solitude so many people had passed this way before. He had stooped to run a hand over the depression, thinking as he did of the stone wall on Wood Island, over in Sheepscot Bay. He had gone out there with Warren Quintaille to make repairs to an English fish carrier that had had a fire. The *Mayflower;* the damage wasn't much, with the day's work she sailed. Jabez hadn't expected any such village as he found there. Snug homes, wharves, derricks, and acres of drying flakes. Men were cutting and salting cod, and others were turning the curing fish on the racks. And Jabez asked about the stone wall up on the crest of the island. A tremendous bit of work. Who built it? What was it for? Nobody knew, except that it had always been there. It was there when the fisheries began. If it were for protection, what had been on Wood Island to defend? To fence animals? What happened so long ago that it was forgotten? And now, how many feet had stepped precisely here for how many centuries to cause this hollow in the ledge? Jabez, having found Morning River, was not the first. And now Jules introduced two men who had come over that long trail. Jules had known them back in Acadia. Father Bois spoke perfect English; Naddah never spoke anything. Naddah made a lean-to by the upper falls, and Father Bois caught his trout. While he was at it, Naddah fixed a smokehouse, and made a basket for carrying smoked trouts back to Lac Raffine. They came each spring for some years, and then came no more. One year they had stayed nearly a month so Naddah could show Jules how to shape the skin on a canoe, and Jabez had jested that a priest away from his flock so long was probably of little esteem. This drew the question: "You are alone here for many years—is there a reason?"

It was in May, on Elzada's second birthday, that

Naddah the Micmac came once more over the "long trail." He came alone, to sign that Father Bois had been gathered. Very old and very tired, he came out of the woods to be discovered by Martha. Jabez, down by the mill, heard her scream of terror and ran. She was on her knees on the ground, hands to her face, staring at Naddah the Micmac, seared with fright. Jabez saw that Naddah the Micmac was equally unnerved, standing there with no notion of why. Jabez made a motion and Naddah moved on to the Marcoux house. Jabez lifted Martha to her feet.

"It's all right!" he said.

She gasped, "Indian!"

"Yes, it's all right. He's an old friend. It's all right!"

When Jabez got Martha to the house and in bed he gave her a jolt of cellar rum, which quieted her somewhat, and then he told her about Father Bois and Naddah and the long trail. She wasn't herself for a couple of days. Naddah spent one night in the place of his lean-to and was gone. He never came again, and was the last of his people ever to come over the old trail. Martha, pioneer of the Maine wilderness, where Indians roamed by the thousands, never saw but two in her life. She told Elzada long afterward, "Gave me one hell of a start! And sure spoilt your birthday!"

That was in May, and as Jabez comforted his wife after her fright, he came to have his first son, David. Then, almost two years apart to the day came Gordon, Grant, and Naomi. Naomi didn't live long, and Jabez and Jules made the first grave at Morning River Farm, laying in the tiny pine box that Jules had fashioned in the boatshop. So there was Elzada growing up with three younger brothers, and Marie-Paule adroitly instructing her in the wily feminine arts of how to come out on top against odds. Jules said, one time, "She wrap her liddle finger 'round dem, for sure, by god!" Jules was good authority; Marie-Paule had a strong liddle finger, too.

After some time, Jules asked Martha, "No more kid?" Martha said she thought not, that she felt some sort of change when Naomi died. But then, she shrugged, who knows? And since the subject had come up—how about Marie-Paule? No more kid?

"Les oreillons," said Jules.

That evening Martha said to Jabez, "What would Marie-Paule have that Jules would call 'lays or-ry-on'?"

"Damned if I know—when did she have this?"

"I don't know. Jules said she couldn't have more babies because she had the whatever-it-is."

Jabez asked Jules the next day. "What's this disease Marie-Paule had?"

"Marie-Paule? Mon épouse? She never got no disease. Healthy like trout. Who tol' you Marie-Paule sick?"

"You told Martha. Said she couldn't have anymore babies."

"Dat's right. No more kid. Les oreillons." Jules blew out his cheeks and made a gesture under his ears.

"Mumps?"

"Maybe. Big here, mumps—si."

"When did Marie-Paule have the mumps?"

"Marie-Paule? I tol' you, Marie-Paule never 'ave sick day on top her life. Me, I'm got mumps. Sick like hell. No more baby now for Marie-Paule."

When Jabez explained to Martha, she said, "Then am I correct, Mr. Knight—you never had the mumps?"

"I can prove it," said Jabez.

At breakfast Martha said, "If I'm not up a stump after last night, we can assume I'm past childbirth." Then, "But you keep trying!"

"Damn right," said Jabez.

4

The Marcoux children had left Morning River. Years before, looking ahead, Marie-Paule had made arrangements with Father Bois for Cécile to attend a sisters' school, and hardly more than a child she had sailed, after a tearful farewell, on the coaster to Fundy, never to return. She finished school and married, and then no more was heard. 'Tit Jules, having learned to operate the sawmill, set himself up as a lumber dealer, and offered scoots and scantlings to passing vessels. A schooner could be well loaded below, but still have room for some boards on deck to increase the profits of a voyage. One skipper, taking some boards, told of a mill being set up on the Saint John—that would be the Saint Jean to 'Tit Jules— and a sawyer was needed. 'Tit Jules went to Canada, prospered, and soon sent for Omar. Neither of the boys ever came back to Morning River.

Going back, it was the year Elzada was born in May that the first warship came to Morning River. In July. Jabez looked out the bedroom window at daybreak and saw her anchored over on the Long Razor side. He picked

Elzada from her cradle and tucked her into bed with her mother, and then went to find Jules. The warship couldn't be seen from Jules's level, so up the two men came into the bedroom to look. Martha was sitting on the edge of the bed with Elzada at her breast, and she said, "My god! For a parade like this you should have musicians!" Jules turned, saw, and took off his cap. But he turned to the window, and there she was—big in the dawn, and much too big to come up the estuary. Then a landing boat came up the river, walking on long sweeps that kept rhythm. Jules and Jabez were at the wharf when the seamen elevated oars and the craft glided smoothly until Jules could take the painter. He made a hitch, and turned to whisper to Jabez, "Frenchmens!"

The conversation between Jules and the young officer conveyed nothing to Jabez. But he could see that Jules was handling things nicely, and he believed his hearty "Bonjour! B'envenu!" had surprised the visitors. They had supposed this an English outpost, and had come to destroy it. To be welcomed in their own language made a big difference. It was to be some time before Jabez and Martha learned what this was all about, but for now they went along with Jules. And Marie-Paule—Marie-Paule made a massive creamed codfish and served it to the seamen under the trees, and as Jules, Jabez, and Martha entertained the officer up at the big house, they could hear Marie-Paule's clear soprano above the rousing male chorus of "Ma 'tite chérie au port de mer." You name it and Marie-Paule would sing it. "My god!" said Martha. "At breakfast!" She had finished with Elzada, dressed, and had now drawn embers forth on the hearth to prepare hospitality. She listened to Jules and the officer, but like Jabez, she understood nothing. After the first round of cellar rum, their conversation bloomed, and she guessed that Jules was thumping the officer on the back in appreciation of a well-told drollery. Jules had things well in hand.

The longboat pulled away after a jolly forenoon, the officer making a handsome salute, and the warship sailed before evening. Jules tried valiantly to explain the reason for the visit, but failed. Nearly two weeks later an English sloop called, and the skipper gave Jabez the answers. He had just come from Cross Island, down near Skitchwak, and knew the whole story. Phinney Vines, a reformed pirate out of The Saco, had persuaded some Boston moneylenders to set him up in business at Cross Island. This was well down in Passamaquoddy lands, and a likely spot. Beaver, mostly. So this trading post was booming, and it was in the heart of the Frenchman's New France. Now Jabez remembered that Jules and the officer had spoken of "Acadie" often in their conversation. Well, the fat was in the fire! The boss of the works at Port Royal heard about this and didn't like it a little bit! The king of France had given this land to him, to Claude de la Tour! So Claude goes to Skitchwak, knocks off some of the Englishmen, takes the rest prisoner, steals what he can—mostly beaver pelts—and sets fire to everything that will burn. He goes back to Port Royal thinking he's done a good day's work. The Englishmen never had a chance.

"I touched in there a few days later," said the slooper, "and it wasn't a pretty sight. I got the rest of the story afterwards. This Vines insists that somebody rescue his men and teach the frogs a lesson, and the Boston money almost brought this off. But somebody decided to send an agent in peace and see if the trouble couldn't be settled with a crooked finger over a teacup.

"Nothing doing. This agent does his best, and asks

politely if he may see the papers under which La Tour
carries on these bothersome and unfriendly acts. La Tour
goes into a tanty. 'Papers, my eye!' he says. 'The only
papers I got is this here,' and he wallops a sword he's
got on his belt. He says, 'If you Englishmen come east
of Pemaquid again, you'll be invading France and making a big mistake! Now, go home!' So the agent went
home. Didn't even get the prisoners. That's the last I
heard, but it explains the warship. If you hadn't had
this Frenchman to talk for you, you'd be far away right
now. I believe it. This won't be any country around
here for Englishmen."

A day or so later Jules said he was going to Port Royal.
He would be gone a while. He needed some French
money, and a description of the Morning River property. Jabez had difficulty following his words, but thanks
to his gestures Jules prevailed. Jabez wrote the description, following his English deed but not setting down
anything that would betray its origin. Jules had been
able to convey that in Port Royal they would not take
kindly to an English deed. In the *Elzada*, Jules rode an
outgoing tide and beyond the gooseneck he ran up sail
and caught a breeze. He might be no more than one
night at sea. He caught the tiller between his knees and
opened the *panier* Marie-Paule had packed with food.
He laid a chicken *hanche* on the stern sheets, with some
bread and cheese, and he drew the cork on a bottle of
blackberry wine. Now off Outer Razor Island, he saw
the mains'l was drawing, as he and Jabez had meant it
to, and as he was now out of sight of home, he knew
Marie-Paule had stopped watching and was in the house.

Jules was gone almost a month. The *Elzada* appeared
in mid-morning, rode daintily up the estuary, and Jules
hove a line to Jabez. Neither spoke. Marie-Paule came

running down, smothered Jules, and still no word had been spoken. Jules handed some things from the *Elzada* to Jabez on the wharf, and then he said, "Bimeby."

When "bimeby" came, Jules and Jabez were at the big house and Martha had made them flip. Marie-Paule came and sat close to Jules on his bench. Jules opened a pouch and handed Jabez a parchment document, rolled and tied with a royal purple ribbon. "Dat's deed," he said. Jabez couldn't read the French, so Jules went back into the pouch and brought out an English translation, made for him by the curé. Jabez read a few words and then things dawned for him. He knew why Jules had gone to Port Royal. Here, under the hand of Claude de la Tour, with the authority of the Royal Grant of Henri IV to Pierre du Guast, Sieur de Monts, and by him surrendered anno Domini 1613 to Madame de Guercheville, was a deed to Morning River. The bounds were identical with those he had copied from his English deed except for one thing—the French gave to low water mark, the English stopped at "mean high tide."

Jabez let this sink in. He saw that the deed was not made out to Jules Marcoux, as it might well have been, but delivered "for value received" to Jabez Knight of Acadie. "You had to pay for this, Jules?"

"But not much, My ver' good friend, la Tour, was remember good time here wit' Marie-Paule for sing h'all doze Franch song. An' look here on your new name!" He pointed at a line in the French deed. There was the name, "Jephté Bellenuit."

"He's you," said Jules, "brudder to Marie-Paule Marcoux!"

"I don't believe one damn' word of it," said Martha. "I'd never let Jules Marcoux marry my sister-in-law."

"Comment?" asked Jules.

Jabez said, "But Jules, if we're challenged, I can't prove anything by this!"

"No need. Look . . ." He handed Jabez a birth certificate showing that one Jephté Bellenuit was born in Avignon in 1594, baptized in the cathedral of Nôtre Dame des Doms. The next sheet of paper attested that Jephté Bellenuit was known by the undersigned to be one and the same with Jabez Knight, witness the hand of Claude de la Tour, Commandant, Port Royal, New France. The curé had translated.

And the last document in Jules's pouch was a marine charter for the *Elzada*, registered at Port Royal as a French vessel engaged in the king's service with a warrant to draw on the provincial treasury not to exceed five *livres tournois* a year.

"Jesus to Jesus!" said Martha.

Marie-Paule made the sign of the cross.

5

Jules had fully expected some repercussions to the French-English to-do down Machias way, and was sure there would be need for the papers he brought back from Port Royal. If the English came, Jabez could do the talking. But there were no repercussions—at least at Morning Farm. Each year more and more vessels passed along the coast, and more than a few of them paused to run in at Morning River. Jabez and Martha heard of disturbances, but none came near. Manny the Portygee, over on Outer Razor, had found two men to help him and now had a fish-curing business. Jabez fixed some poles and Marie-Paule made some flags, and they now had a signal arrangement. Run up a flag and Manny or his men would come over; Manny would run up his flag if a passing boat left something for Morning River with him. One of the men on Outer Razor had a wife, and one day Manny the Portygee came to tell them that she had a broken leg and they had to shoot her. "That's not funny," said Martha.

"No, and it's not true," said Jabez, "but a hundred

years from now they'll be telling wild stories like that about us foolish far-downers. But anyway, don't go breaking a leg."

Marie-Paule had quite a few books, and now Martha began sending for books. It wasn't a matter of asking for anything in particular; it was just "bring some books." As boats paused on their way, enough books came so Jabez shelved a back room, and Morning River had a library. Elzada was indeed competent in two languages by the time she was six, and in the next few years she learned to read both. The French books came from the east'ard and the English books from Boston, and one day a book came that said, "Printed in Boston." Martha and Marie-Paule both heard daily lessons, and Marie-Paule made all the children memorize the catechism—in French. Elzada turned ten, and on her birthday Martha said, "She should go somewhere to school."

"I'd thought of that. It would probably mean England. Jules and Marie-Paule sent Cécile down east."

"Must be some way to get her into a family somewhere to go to a real school. See what you can find out."

So Jabez told Manny, and Manny told passing captains, and in a few weeks every English settlement from Pemaquid to Providence wanted a little girl from away up the coast to come and live and go to school. All summer letters came telling how much a week, a month, a term, and Elzada kept saying she didn't want to go away to school, and wouldn't.

That was the summer Jabez did some work on the aging *Elzada* and fixed her up to take his family on a cruise. To find if there was room, they anchored overnight on the Long Razor Island side, and they decided they could be comfortable. Then they came by the wind in two days to Monhegan Island. The next day Jabez ran the *Elzada* up the bay to Bristol, found it little changed, and kept his thoughts to himself. He didn't go ashore. But he did hug Elzada close against his hip, and he said, "Some women get boats named for 'em—bet you're the only young lady ever got named for a boat!"

Overhearing, Martha said, "Under the circumstances, it was a fine idea."

Jabez was astonished at the number and size of the villages they passed. Just ten years, and the country was filling up. Monhegan was about the same, but Pemaquid was booming. He took his family to the Damariscoves and pointed out the stone walls on Wood Island. He saw many sails at the Sagadahock, and again at the New Meadows. The family dallied at the Aucocisco Islands for two days. Falmouth wasn't much, but Scarborough looked prosperous. The *Elzada* paused in turn at Saco, Wells, York, Isles of Shoals, and then Jabez jogged for the tide to turn off the Piscataqua. It did, and the *Elzada* was sucked up past Pull-and-be-damned—there she was, tying up once more at Strawberry Banke. Jabez and Martha stood with their arms around each other, looking up at the town. She snuggled against his hip and stood a-tiptoe to whisper, "What would you hosey right now except for four youngsters in the way?"

He lifted his hand from her waist, cupped it a little higher, and said, "Bunny Rabbit!"

Martha said, "I owe you one."

The ceremonial flips they had at the inn led to inquiries about a family where Elzada might fit in and go to school. But Elzada overheard, repeated that she would not leave home to go to school, and she spoke so firmly the subject never came up again.

The *Elzada* scooted to Morning River in jig time, and the vacation was over.

6

Wherever the *Elzada* stopped on that cruise, the summer of 1643, people asked Jabez, as soon as they knew he was from the east'ard, about the tensions in New France. Truth was, they seemed to know more about them than he, so he picked up considerable gossip to take back to Jules Marcoux. Seems the governor of New France, Razilla, had died, leaving two of his generals to squabble over his job. The king of France was having a dandy little war with the king of Spain, and took small interest in what happened in Acadia. He left Charles de la Tour (not Jules's friend Claude) and D'Aulney de Charnisy, the two generals, to their own devices. De la Tour set himself up at the mouth of the Saint John River, with a big fort, and declared himself governor. D'Aulney did the same at Mount Desert Island, with a branch office at the Bagaduce—not too far from Morning River. De la Tour was a Protestant; D'Aulney was not. The Jesuits, playing so big a role in the affairs of *l'Acadie*, prayed on the side of D'Aulney and never doubted but God would sustain their cause. De la Tour thought he had a better idea, so he went to Boston and conferred with the moneylenders. He needed money, ships, men, and encouragement. In return, he offered peace and open trade.

The Bostonians considered this carefully. Hmmmmmm . . . On the one hand . . . Of course, neither this chap Tour and the other chap, there—what's his name?—D'Aulney, speaks with the king of France behind him. On the other hand . . . The possibilities are attractive. After due reflection they told de la Tour that they could not possibly involve themselves, or any English influences, in his cause, but that he was at liberty to charter vessels, recruit men, and buy arms and supplies—how much credit did he require and what was his collateral? De la Tour was far from an idiot, and as he had asked the Boston gentlemen for a great deal more than he needed, he got what he expected. He mortgaged his fort on the Saint John for the few thousands required, picked out his vessels, and hired 142 men from the Boston docks to his work. Artful equivocation spared the Boston bankers the charge of meddling in foreign matters, and as they watched the squadron of de la Tour sail from the harbor, one of them rubbed his hands and said, "We can't lose!"

But any and all of the settlers between Boston and Arichat could lose, and as Jabez made his holiday cruise he became aware of mistrust. From Morning River, nobody saw the five vessels of the de la Tour fleet pass to the east'ard; it was within the week that Jabez and his family passed to the west'ard in the *Elzada*. Everywhere he stopped Jabez met uneasiness—the Boston bankers getting us involved in who knows what?

De la Tour won the first round. He drove D'Aulney off Mount Desert. Two of D'Aulney's ships went aground and the third was captured. D'Aulney got to the Bagaduce, and some of his men got to Port Royal. The ship de la Tour captured was loaded with beaver skins, so he smiled a lot as he took her to Boston to pay off the bankers. The whole foray had taken two months, de la Tour was governor, the Boston bankers made out fine, and for a time tensions eased along The Maine.

The rest of this great moment in history is a dandy plot for a comic opera. D'Aulney was not discouraged. He blustered a good bit about what he was going to do, and laid plans for a return bout. He got the ear of the French king, thanks to the Jesuits, and the king denounced de la Tour, outlawing him and his wife. She was a gracious lady of much beauty and had a head on her shoulders, a personage much neglected in the lore of outlaws. D'Aulney returned to sack Saint John, de la Tour was deposed and ruined, and Mme. de la Tour was a prisoner of D'Aulney, never to see her husband again.

It turned out, however, to be tit for tat. When D'Aulney died, de la Tour showed up again, appealed again to his friends in Boston, and was outfitted again—this time to trade and traffic along The Maine. The agitation of the long disturbance subsided, and the open trade de la Tour had promised was a fact. The pleasant touch of the story is that de la Tour married D'Aulney's widow and, as Jules Marcoux would have put it, ". . . 'ad fo-fi' kid."

As Jules Marcoux also put it when Jabez came back from the cruise and tried to explain the matter, "Why was dey be such damn fool?"

7

After these playful capers in New France, contributing
to the jitters all along the coast, New England experienced the same kind of absentee neglect. With civil war,
England was all up in a heaval, and petition as they did,
nobody in The Maine, or in Boston for that matter, got
much attention. Massachusetts had extended her influ-
ence up the coast and the pattern of the future was laid
out. The Maine continued to have four distinct sec-
tions, the fourth of which was the far-down Penobscot
area, the location of Morning River. It was a kind of
buffer between New France and New England. Well,
in the beginning the French thought of New France as
roughly the same place the English considered New
England—some of the early descriptions amounted to
everything from Newfoundland to just about Philadel-
phia, and thence to the westward ocean. Certainly from
Nova Scotia to New York. But the old Plymouth Company, from which Jabez Knight held his English deed,
had petered out rather much to the claims of the Gorges
heirs who now felt they were entitled to York County,

of The Maine—Yorkshire. But they got disputes on that, from Massachusetts. Interesting that in 1648 some jittery Mainers wrote to England asking for advice and instruction. They certainly were not too aware of matters there. King Charles was being held in escrow, the second civil war was hatching, and Cromwell, having joined the army, was riding about on three horses at once. The historian says it took over a year to get a reply, and the Mainers might as well have saved postage. Charles I, friend of Sir Ferdinando Gorges—Gorges had died recently—was beheaded on January 30, 1649, even while his loyal subjects in The Maine were waiting for his answer. However, in spite of the upheaval in England, a great many people along The Maine were disenchanted with the irrational way they were being handled by England, and actually returned there. Enough so the Massachusetts colony sought to straighten things out, and sent its agents with "the oath."

It was now that the second warship came to Morning River. She anchored in about the same place over by Long Razor and again a landing boat came up the estuary. "English!" Jules said, and he was right. Jabez welcomed the landing boat.

"Oh," said the man in the bow, "we had presumed you to be French!"

"You're welcome, just the same—please come ashore and enjoy the beauty of Morning River!"

"Lovely place," the man said. He looked back over the ocean. "Lovely. Brian Pendleton at your service, agent of the governor, Land Claims Commission, Boston."

"Jabez Knight—and this is my friend and partner, Julius Martin."

Jules ducked his head, he was not about to "speak

som'ting troo d'mout." But he and Jabez knew that a day was at hand which Jules had foreseen long ago. English or French, let 'em come! The strongbox had everything. So now Marie-Paule made another big creamed codfish and the oarsmen tackled it under the trees. Elzada, this time, helped serve, and contrived to shield Marie-Paule so she had no reason to speak. Up at the big house, Martha had made flip and was getting a meal. Agent Pendleton was explaining things to Jabez.

Since the French disturbance down east, and the death of Gorges with resulting confusion, there had been talk along The Maine of an independent government. It made more sense, thought Massachusetts, for Massachusetts to step in and take over. So with authority to confirm land titles in The Maine, Pendleton and his colleagues were doing what they could. Pendleton happened to mention that with Oliver Cromwell doing so well, the Puritan complexion of Boston was rosy indeed. He trusted, with a question mark, that the property here was covered by an adequate deed?

"Yes," said Jabez. "I have a deed, but are we in any hurry?"

"Not at all. Indeed, this teases me to linger. What is it?"

"That's flip," said Martha.

"Flip'?"

"Flip. Let me fill your mug."

Jabez didn't explain that the best flip is made with rum off a French boat. Jules did that dickering, and it was shameful how few boards it took to get a pipe of excellent rum after a skipper had taken hospitality at Marie-Paule's table.

"Never heard of flip. What's in it?"

"Just the right amount of everything," said Martha.

"If you've never had flip, you haven't seen too much of The Maine."

"Quite otherwise," said Pendleton. "I've been all summer along the coast, holding meetings in every settlement."

The eyes of Jabez and Martha met. If this man had been to every settlement in The Maine and hadn't been offered a flip until Morning River—must be something about him. Jabez decided to be cozy.

"I never had any business with Boston," he began. "Been as far west as The Piscataqua, is all. Nobody from Boston comes here—except schooner captains, and they could just as well be from some place else. Have the people along The Maine cottoned to you? How do they feel about Massachusetts?"

Agent Pendleton studied his flip. "There is a reluctance. Even antagonism. Yes. But things are rather open and shut—protection of this coast, right now, can best be offered by Massachusetts. Where else can you turn? The French plan to stay, and they claim this land. The Indians are restless. I can't for the life of me understand why people along The Maine are so upset by the oath."

"The oath?"

"The landowners of Maine must agree to support the authority of the Massachusetts Colony. It's as simple as that."

"But I guess it isn't," said Jabez. "We don't have too many worries here at Morning River, but if some kind of trouble comes up, I'd be glad to have some help. I'm willing to do my part. But if folks along the coast aren't going for your proposition, there must be something the matter with it. What's this *oath*?"

"To support Massachusetts. Property is forfeit unless the oath is taken."

"There's a catch, else people would be glad. I'm beginning to understand. You want to make me a Congregationalist?"

"You're right—that's the objection."

"But, Mr. Pendleton . . . "

"Brian. I think flip imposes informality."

"Let me fill your mug again."

"But Brian," Jabez began again. "You're horning in where government has no business to be. That's been the whole trouble with Massachusetts since the beginning—and I was here before Massachusetts was. Most people in Maine came here because they didn't want to live in Massachusetts. My people were established church—if they'd wanted to go to Massachusetts they'd have got a big, fat no. My wife here, Martha, was fetched up Catholic—we hadn't been married a week when she asked me if I believed in transubstantiation. I never heard of it. She says that's a big thing. Neither of us has had a thing to do with a church since we were little . . ."

Jabez broke off abruptly. He had a flash back of Jules coming home from Port Royal with proof that Jephté Bellenuit was baptized in Avignon. He collected himself and went on.

". . . and how would you expect us to? We held hands and married ourselves—where was a priest or a minister? We lost a daughter—she's buried yonder—and who was to pray for her except ourselves? We prayed for her, and I'm damned if I can say what faith we used. Nothing Massachusetts would favor, but here on The Maine it suited us fine. No, you're off course there."

Martha said, "It comes to me that you're a long ways from the people who sent you. I mean, suppose I signed up to go to your church—where would I go? We can take twenty oaths and be no nearer to a pulpit. There's

been many a time, I can tell you, that I've had a mind
to go to church and have somebody pray for me, but by
the time I ever got down to Boston the fit would-a passed.
Tell me, Mr. Pendleton, are *you* a Congregationalist?"

Pendleton sighed. "It's just a formality! I don't
understand! Why, there was one man down in Yorkshire who absolutely made a scene. Nasty scene. Cursed
most abusive profanity, even one of my sailors blushed.
True, he then up and took the oath without a qualm.
The thing to do. You might say he was over a barrel."

"Martha, you're over a barrel!" Then, to Pendleton,
"I have no objections at all to taking your oath if that
confirms my ownership of this land, and if it's going to
bring me help if I need any. But that isn't going to make
me a Boston Congregationalist, and I'll bet you another
mug of flip that boy down in Yorkshire had his fingers
crossed so hard his knuckles were blue."

Martha filled the mug.

"Thank you, Mrs. Knight!"

"Only Congregationalists get to call me Mrs. Knight,
and I only serve flip to my friends. Food is ready; please
to sit here Brian?"

Expecting to find French settlers, Pendleton had not
brought his satchel ashore, so the seamen were sent to
the vessel to fetch it, and it was well into the afternoon,
with Martha's chicken pie well settled, that the cere-
mony took place. Two sailors were witnesses, and Jabez
and Martha Knight of Morning River Quadrangle, Penobscot Jurisdiction, Province of Maine, became devout
and recorded Boston Separatists. Jabez wished he could
think of some way to get Jules Marcoux onto the paper—
to pay him back for that baptism in Avignon.

Pendleton said the Plymouth Company deed was in
order, and confirmation at Boston would be routine.

Copies of all Plymouth Company deeds were on file, so no need to make another. Massachusetts, Pendleton suggested, had been making ready to annex the rest of North Virginia. Jabez's title was sound as a nut.

Jabez didn't show Pendleton the French deed from Port Royal.

Jules was halfway to the barn for the evening milking when Pendleton was rowed down the estuary. His ship sailed at once, turning around Outer Razor to go farther down east. "Ver' few Bostons that way," he thought. Just as Pendleton's vessel got under way Jules saw a puff of white smoke at the fantail. It was a minute or so before the sound of the signal gun reached him.

8

When the three Knight boys were old enough, each, in turn, went to sea. Jabez and Jules, the boys helping, made each of them a schooner. All lofted alike, they were launched the *Martha*, the *Elzada II*, and the *Marie-Paule*. For a few years the boys would touch in at Morning River, always with just barely time enough to say hello and be off. For some years now nothing had been heard of them; no more the Marcoux children. Jabez and Martha, hale and active, had Elzada with them, and Elzada, unwed but happy, wanted only to stay at Morning Farm. Except for day sails, usually with Jules after some fish, she had left Morning Farm only for the family cruise to Strawberry Banke—now long ago. Jules and Marie-Paule kept well, and little by little the affairs of Morning Farm tapered off so there was little to do. The big gardens were a thing of the past, and the latest yoke of steers had been beefed, smoked, salted, and eaten. Jules still kept a cow, and Marie-Paule made butter and cheese. Marie-Paule and Martha kept their youth, both lovely women. And Elzada, now past thirty, had her

mother's good features and her father's lithe figure. Some
might have called her "stringy," but never so stringy as
to be unattractive. Elzada was quite all right. The boatshop kept ready to do small work as it came along, but
Jules and Jabez attempted no large construction after
the *Marie-Paule* was launched. The grist mill and the
sawmill were used only when somebody came by boat
and did his own work. From Jabez's first boat repairs,
back even before Jules joined him, there had always been
money flowing toward Morning Farm and so little to
spend it for. When a passing boat did bring something
that must be paid for, Morning Farm usually had something to swap. Jabez had his steel strongbox in a secret
place. One day he showed Elzada where it was.

Jabez was seventy-three. Jules made his casket, working all night by a bonfire, and in the morning dug the
farm's second grave. The third was for Martha, who
lived just one month after Jabez left her. Jabez's will, in
his own handwriting and assented to by Martha, left
Morning River Farm and all effects to Elzada. "Subject
only," it said, "to the life interest of Jules Marcoux, as
otherwise provided." Elzada had known about that
agreement. Jules lived through the next winter, attending the cow and doing little else except playing his violin. Like Jabez, he was hearty to the end—they were
just hardy old seed stock who came to the end of their
books. The Maine saying is, "They got through." Marie-
Paule came up to the big house to tell that Jules had
gone. "Le drapeau," she said. "Jules est mort." Her eyes
were dry. The two islanders came later in the day—
wound Jules in sailcloth, and dug another grave. Elzada
thought the small bundle, a corner moving in the breeze,
looked pitifully small to contain a man who had meant
so very much. The sky was bright. The upper cascade

of Morning River made its requiem. Marie-Paule stood apart, looking to the hills, her hands clasped at her breast. The two islanders leaned on shovels. Elzada, half aloud and half to herself, began to repeat the catechism as she had learned it—in French. At the first question, Marie-Paule crossed herself, and seeing her do it the islanders looked at each other. Then they bent their ears to listen to Elzada—they hadn't known she spoke *that!* But she ran on only a minute; Marie-Paule stepped up to say, "Ça suffit; il est tranquille; merci." She turned away, still dry-eyed, and Elzada nodded at the islanders.

As Martha with Jabez, so Marie-Paule with Jules. Three days later she didn't come to the big house, and Elzada found her in her rocking chair by the window— dressed, she hadn't gone to bed the evening before. Elzada raised the signal flag and this time Manny the Portygee came—the islanders were at sea. He dug Marie-Paule's grave, and Elzada helped him carry Marie-Paule to it. Before the Portygee went back to the island he lowered the signal flag, folded it, handed it to Elzada.

"When you need me," he said.

So there you have it. Morning Farm; Elzada all soul alone with Jules's cow to milk. She sat the next morning at her kitchen table with her father's strongbox open, and with a similar box she had found in the Marcoux house. In Jule's box she found the half-interest paper; his interest reverted to Jabez when he died. There was no provision for Marie-Paule, none for the Marcoux children. In Jules's box she found a considerable collection of coins; he had left a substantial fortune. French and English, mostly, but some Spanish, Portuguese, and some Elzada didn't recognize. In her father's box she found a great many more coins than Jules had left— some Dutch. Wonder why Jules didn't have any Dutch

coins? Then she found the two deeds, and she read them
carefully before taking up the next paper. That was a
memorandum of the visit by Brian Pendleton, and Pendleton had signed it. Jabez had been thoughtful. There
was a copy of his agreement with Jules. There were
memoranda of the marriage of Jabez and Martha, of the
births of the five children, the foolish birth certificate
from Avignon, and a note about the death of Naomi.
Then the coins. Elzada brought the ink and rounded
out the records with circumstances and dates about her
father and mother, and about the Marcoux. She put
things back in the boxes, put the boxes on a shelf in the
mudroom, and then went to stand at the window and
look out for a long time.

Morning River Farm was all hers. But she was alone.
What now?

9

The Morning River cow that Elzada now attended as the latest-left of the farm chores was named Fannie, and she was elderly. Best Elzada could guess, she was about twenty when Jules brought Fannie from Port Royal, and Jules had been gone on that errand a long time. As he told Marie-Paule the details of his adventure, Elzada became well informed on the subject of procreation, and learned a good many new French words. Fannie, then a heifer, had not been bred, and as Morning River had no bull, it was imprudent to bring Fannie home until she was. Copulation is essential to the flow of milk, and the physical rhythm of a cow must be heeded if cream, milk, and cheese are to be provided. There was great inconvenience about all this at Morning River, and Jules had always procrastinated with the previous cows. Well, at a reasonable period before a bossie's maternal urge, he would have to position her, sling her, hoist her, and lower her all a-blat aboard the sloop, allowing time to get her to Fundy for an assignation. Then he had to get her ashore, and after *l'amour* he would have to repeat

57

everything to bring her home. Cattle are poor sailors.
So Jules had little trouble thinking of something else to
do when his cow was in need, and usually she would
be so dried out that she would wince when he squeezed,
and often celibacy prevailed until Morning Farm was
without dairy products. Besides, the remote location of
Morning Farm caused a cow to linger beyond normal
years, and now as Elzada sat on the stool patiently coax-
ing Fannie, she reflected that the poor beast must be at
least twenty-two years old.

It was about twenty years ago that Jules went to buy
her. The cow she replaced had given up. Jules found
her at Chignecto, liked the looks of her, haggled, and
bought her. The deal hinged on her being bred, and he
and the other man took Fannie behind the barn and
introduced her to a bull in a pen. Jules explained to
Marie-Paule that Fannie was perhaps a trifle young, and
seemed not to know why she was there. Elzada was all
ears.

But the bull, said Jules, was also on the youthful side,
and small at that, and at first look he had told the other
man they were wasting everybody's time. Maybe not,
said the man, let's try it anyway. The other man and
Jules had extended the happy couple every encouragement, but a conjugal fruition had not resulted. Elzada
heard. The other man suggested they wait and try
tomorrow, and for almost a month Jules and the other
man had led Fannie to the pen, and as Fannie continued
to show reluctance, the young bull would look apart
and walk away. Jules could only sit around and wait,
so he sat around and waited. Every day they tried again,
and Jules related to Marie-Paule the variety of entice-
ments, cajoleries, and artifices they had resorted to in
their effort to mate the beasts. Then, said Jules, one

morning Fannie was willing, the bull was ready, and he could go home. Elzada remembered all this as she stripped poor Fannie, and after she set the small pan of Fannie's residual milk on the cool cellar floor, she raised the signal flag.

Manny and the two islanders came at once, and Elzada beckoned them to the big house where she had the flip ready. First, they decided to slaughter Fannie at Morning Farm, and carry her in quarters to Outer Razor, where they would cure her in the fish smoke-house. Elzada told them to divide four ways. Next Elzada wanted to go to Boston. Would they pass the word and have a suitable vessel come to pick her up? Raise the signal flag, and she would be ready when the boat came up the estuary. She charged them to keep an eye on Morning Farm, and to use the mill and the boatshop if they wished. "I expect to be in Boston some time, but if things go well, perhaps not. But I'll be back one day, and I want you to keep things ready for me."

They lifted their flip mugs in agreement, and after another round they went to the island. They would come early tomorrow to attend to Fannie.

Elzada's ride to Boston appeared sooner than she expected, and 'twas a happy surprise. Captain Alonzo Plaice of the schooner *Madrigal* got the word from Manny, and came right across. Elzada hadn't seen the signal flag, and she was surprised at Captain Plaice's thump on her door. He had sent his two-man crew to anchor the *Madrigal* outside and wait. He took Elzada's hands, kissed her lightly on the forehead, and offered condolences. "Manny tells me you took a browsin'!"

"Oh, 'Lon—I'm all alone! Are you going to take me to the ends of the earth?"

That was going back many years. The first time Captain Plaice had brought the *Madrigal* to Morning River he beached her out while Jabez fitted a new bowsprit. He had either punched an island or something had punched him, but he was close-mouthed about the accident and Jabez never knew. The job took a few days and Captain Plaice stayed ashore at the big house. The first evening, at supper, he had been charmed by Elzada, who was seventeen or eighteen—Captain Plaice must have been at his mid-twenties then—and he exploded, "Migawd! Isn't she something to come home to!" Elzada was hardly ready for the appraising finger he ran along her armpit, and Elzada looked at her mother. Martha had noticed, and she was smiling. Captain Plaice went on, "Lovely girl! Mrs. Knight—may I have the honor of being the first gentleman to propose to your daughter?"

So he had proposed. He said, "I'll seize you, bind you, carry you to my enchanted ship, and we'll sail to the ends of the earth and live happy ever after! Bigawd, I will!"

So there was this small fun, and then Captain Plaice had said, "Only one problem. What do we do about my wife and ten children?"

So Captain Plaice and the *Madrigal* came to Morning River at intervals—he had some business dealings with Manny the Portygee—and he would always bring Elzada some gift, usually books, and he would protest his undying love and ask what to do about his wife and ten children. Except for that first tracing with his finger, he had made no advances until now, when he had kissed her forehead at the door. But Elzada remembered that first touch—caress—and how her mother had smiled. Indeed, that prompted Martha to her motherly duties, and the next day she took Elzada to the bedroom and communicated at length, including all about a finger at the bodice.

The ends of the earth! "I want to go to Boston," she said. "Can you take me?"

" 'Course I can. The *Madrigal* goes there, and we have four berths. I'll move aloft and you take mine below."

"I'm not a stranger to boats."

"We'll use you fine, except that I'm cook. But why Boston? Are you leaving here?"

"Long enough to figure things out. What can I do? I need to find somebody to come here and run the place. Somebody to take care of me, I suppose. The place needs a man, and maybe I can find one."

"A husband?"

"The thought has passed my mind, but I don't think so. It ought to be a young man, either married or going to be, who'll love the place and want to stay a lifetime. Somebody, most of all, congenial about having me around the rest of my days."

Captain Plaice laughed. "I'd take you on, except I don't want no damn' farm in the deal."

"And what would we do about your wife and ten children."

"I wish you luck," he said. "You know that."

"I know. My idea is to find somebody in Boston, probably a solicitor, and then go on from there. 'Lon, did you ever have a wife and ten children?"

"No children. The wife is real enough. She's fat and in England. Boyhood mistake, and my only one. She never gave me a child, nor anybody else. I send her money now and again, but haven't heard about her in years."

At dusk he shoved a skiff out of the boatshop and rowed down to the *Madrigal*. Elzada had said, " 'Lon, you can stay the night here." He had shaken his head. "Let's leave things the way they are. I got no hoseys to own a garden, and I'm scairt of being convinced. Pick you up on the forenoon tide."

Once upon a long-ago time, when Elzada had first come across the lines in a book, she used to repeat them before dropping off to sleep. Wistfully. Afterwards, she would repeat them once in a while just because they stated a fact. Tonight, as she snuggled in bed after 'Lon had rowed off, she repeated them again—and again wistfully:

> The moon is down,
> The Pleiades are set,
> And I lie alone . . .

10

Elzada was standing on the wharf when the *Madrigal* came, towing the skiff. The two boys of Captain 'Lon's crew stowed the skiff in the boatshop and went up to the big house to fetch Elzada's chest. Captain 'Lon had called, before the *Madrigal* touched the wharf, "All ready? First time in my life I never had to wait for a woman!" Then he stepped from the schooner, put his hands on Elzada's hips and held her neither far nor close, so their eyes were even. "I didn't have too good a night," he said.

"Nor I."

"I wanted to stay, but I had to think. I laid awake stewing things over. I may have decided—I hope so. For, I guess I did the right thing. And, for now, welcome aboard! Make a last check; got everything?"

"I think so—except money. I've got money, but I don't know some of the values."

"No problem. I've got money, and I'm known in Boston. Only one thing for you to remember in Boston about money, and don't forget it for one minute—everybody in Boston is a bahstid, if you'll excuse my French."

"Oh, 'Lon—that's not French! In French it's *bâtard*, with a little hat over it; it's much better to call him an *enfant naturel*. Mind your manners!"

"That's a French bastard, these are Boston bahstids." The boys came with the chest, the line was cast off, and the *Madrigal* drifted down toward the sea. Elzada looked back at her property.

It was September, and the season for turning the winds around. Mostly, the air about The Maine moves west to east, or thereabouts, and from the north and east the winds are overstrong for easy sailing. The old "know-theaster" is a bitch, and fetches wild storms that keep the smart seaman in harbor. But in September come soft days with high skies, and a reasonably warm and fresh northeast wind. Not too many of them, but those are the days to be on the water, and this was one of them. Elzada sat on a hatch cover in the sun while Captain 'Lon went ashore on Outer Razor to visit with Manny the Portygee. They had their heads together for a time and while they were talking the crew boys took cargo from Manny's fishing boat and lowered it into the hold of the *Madrigal*. Elzada felt it wasn't fish.

Captain 'Lon was, indeed, the *Madrigal*'s cook. After they'd left Outer Razor behind, he started up his brazier and engineered a stew. Elzada sat on the edge of a berth, and prudently made no offer to help. It would be the skipper's place to give orders. "I'm a sizzler," he told her. "I fry everything except boiled beans and stews. Sometimes things come out pretty good."

"Tell me what you and Manny are about," she said.

"Manny? Well, I guess I can tell you about most anything, and Manny's a good place to start. He fishes the Bank. One time, years ago, I tied up at Arichat, and

Manny came in and tied to me. I had another schooner, the *Moonbeam*, then. Neither Manny nor I knew it, but they were having some kind of a scramble there, and in the morning I hears click-click-click, and along comes a squad of soldiers, straight for the *Moonbeam*. Manny had just cast off and was on his way when I saw this, so with good judgment I grabs up a sack I had and hove it on Manny's deck, yelling to keep it for me, and he's gone. Well, them soldiers went over me with a fine-tooth, keel to truck, and I managed to come up with the idea that they were looking for something they couldn't find. I didn't see Manny for two years, and when I got my sack back it turned out we were good friends."

"Contraband?"

"You might say so."

"What was it?"

"Don't matter now—at that time you could make a penny with just about anything. Taxes. English, French, Dutch—didn't matter. Sell something as if you'd paid the tax, and you got just as much as the king was getting. Kings live well. Manny and I have had our arrangement ever since. Neither one of us does anything wrong, really—it's always the other one."

"And you have the nerve to call people bahstids!"

Captain 'Lon said, "I'd forgotten you speak French. How good is your French?"

"As good as Marie-Paule could make it. And Jules taught me all the dirty words."

"Could be important. Do you think you could walk into a roomful of Frenchmen and get away with it?"

"I know I could."

"Be damned! That may come in handy."

With the friendly northeast wind, the *Madrigal* gained on Boston, and the usual long tacks into a westerly gave way to a good chance-along. The two crew boys took tricks, but it was hardly necessary to touch the tiller. One, the third, afternoon Captain 'Lon motioned for Elzada to take the tiller. He stood beside her, ran an arm about her waist, and held her to him.

"Elzada—'Zadie," he said.

She knew there was no need to say anything.

"I'm sorry about the other night."

Nothing.

"It could have complicated things. Right now, I think we'll work everything out. You see what can be done in Boston. Make an honest try. I'll be somewhere, and I care. Sooner or later I'll check you out. If you don't have an answer by then, remind me."

"And you'll take me to the ends of the earth?"

"Thanks," he said. "Maybe the ends of the earth, but goddamnit, 'Zadie, I don't hanker to spend the rest of my life on a jeezly farm—not even with you!"

"Merci, mon ami—merci mille fois; c'est ça!"

She held the tiller, he held her, and the *Madrigal* sailed smoothly on. One of the crew boys came for his trick.

11

Off Cape Ann the following wind failed and the *Madrigal* had a bad night. Elzada felt the vessel heel, and she didn't come back. Instantly Captain 'Lon's foot hit the edge of Elzada's bunk and he was up the companionway to take the tiller. The two boys trimmed sail, and in ten minutes the *Madrigal* was in a wild westerly squall. The rough sea held until the *Madrigal* was in Boston Harbor the next afternoon. "Been a good sailor," 'Lon told Elzada. "We'll keep you aboard until morning. I've some plans about what to do with you, but first—let's see some of that money you brought."

She emptied a pouch on the table and he poked the coins about. "This all you brought?" he asked, and she said, "No, I've got more in my chest."

"That's good," he said. "You got enough right here to buy Boston. Only trouble is, some of these won't pass here. Take this one—maybe two-three pennies, but in the Loo'ards it'll fetch a pound or more. If you'll trust me, I'll swap." He brought a chest—gave her some of his and took some of hers. "That'll do you a while. I'll be seeing you before you'll need more."

Captain Plaice went ashore after supper and was gone until well after dark. Elzada was in her berth when he came aboard. He sat on the edge, took her hands, kissed them, and told her she was all set. "The tavern isn't the best in Boston, but there's a reason for you to go there. I've signed you in. I signed a paper, too, so if you run out of money don't worry. You're going to wonder now and then why I sent you there, but you'll know one day. We'll settle you in tomorrow morning. The *Madrigal* will most likely be here two days. That's time enough to move you if you think I made a mistake. Now, goodnight 'Zadie, and sweet dreams. I'll bet you inside two weeks you'll have a husband to take back to Morning River!"

He kissed her hands, and smoothed the blanket on her shoulder. "I expect to be back in two weeks."

He was ashore when Elzada woke in the morning. There were sounds and voices from the deck, but as usual she had the cabin to herself while she dressed. She put on a full-skirted woolen suit Marie-Paule had shorn, spun, twisted, dyed, cut, and stitched. Somewhere along the way a bale of Chantilly lace had come to Morning River, and Marie-Paule had used it to advantage. Elzada had no notion of the styles now approved in Boston, but she knew she was attractively dressed, and striking. She came on deck then to meet the stares of some stevedores who hadn't known she was aboard. On sight she had been approved, and she stepped ashore quite ready for Boston.

The two crew boys carried her chest and led the way a short distance up the street to the Golden Clarion. She had never been in a tavern, and had misgivings, but Captain 'Lon had paved the way and the landlord was ready and waiting. "Ah, Mrs. Knight! welcome to the Golden Clarion—your host Rufus Achorn at your service. Your chamber is ready, and I think you'll find my dining room as fine as any in Boston!"

"Thank you, Mr. Achorn, and it's *Miss* Knight."

"*Miss* Knight! A thousand pardons! I wasn't told. Captain Plaice referred only to his friend, *something* Knight from The Maine.

"We're old friends—he may have called me 'Zadie."

"I think he did. But welcome! Will you go to your room now, Miss Knight?"

"Not right away. Coming ashore after the voyage makes me think I'd like a flip."

"A *flip?*"

"A flip. Yes, a flip."

"A *what?*"

"Come, come, Mr. Achorn. Don't you serve a flip?"

"Not by that name anyway. You have the advantage of me."

"Well, I can tell you this, then—that without flip Boston will never amount to a hill of beans."

"I'm sorry."

"It's nothing can't be remedied. Do you have rum?"

"Certainly."

"Sugar? Cream? Eggs?"

"Yes."

"Ale?"

"Oh, yes!"

"Would you like me to show you?"

Achorn didn't seem easy at this, but he led Elzada into the kitchen and produced her ingredients. She wiped the poker and shoved it into the embers on the hearth. She frothed the eggs, sugar, and milk into a pewter pitcher, added ale and rum, and stirred with the hot poker. Mr. Achorn whiffed the result, and took on the expression of a devout monk who has just witnessed another miracle. "That's flip," she told him, "and now we need two mugs." She pulled a stool to the cookery table and sat down. "Down Maine, we always say the kitchen is the best room in the house—will you join me, Mr. Achorn?"

Mr. Achorn sipped and made a wry face, but almost at once the warm pungency flowed through his soul and he was convinced.

After Elzada was in her room and was comfortably relaxed with a second flip, she fell to wondering about Mr. Achorn. There was something about him. Elusive. Captain 'Lon had said there was a reason for her to stay at the Golden Clarion. What reason? What *was* there about Achorn? Was she imagining? Complicity? Intrigue? Captain 'Lon admitted to smuggling. What? All the same, there was something about Mr. Achorn— something artificial. "Achorn?"

It was like the snapping of a whip. Of course! The way he said certain words. Certain words he used. His expressions, his gestures. She should have realized immediately.

She stepped from her room into the corridor, laid a hand on the bannister at the top of the stairs, and loudly—she knew only she and Achorn were in the tavern—she called down, "Ah! M'sieur Aucoin! S'il vous plaît—encore un flip, oui?"

She'd guessed right. Instantly, and in great perturbation, Achorn came to the foot of the stairs with a finger to his lips, and barely loud enough for Elzada to hear he said, "Pas si fort!"

So what might all this be about?

She returned to her room, and Rufus Achorn brought

her another flip—and one for himself. She had left the door open, but he closed it. "We must be careful," she said. But, about what?

She lifted one of the mugs and began the ancient toast: "À ta santé, M'sieur!"

"Et à la tienne! Why must we be careful?

"I haven't any idea. What's this all about? Why the Achorn?"

"Did Captain Plaice tell you about me?"

"He didn't have to. I speak French."

"You live on The Maine. Are you *acadien?*"

"No."

"Have you a message for me?"

"None, except that you put too much sweet'ner in your flip."

"I will learn. But please, Miss Knight, spare me the French in Boston. I am not in danger, but I could be embarrassed if I were asked certain questions. And it might embarrass Captain Plaice!"

"Touché, and an anchor to wind'ard. Now, I stumbled on some kind of ticklish spot, I gather, and I have no idea what it is. I'm here on my own business, and not yours, and not of Captain Plaice. Fear not that I am with you! Now, can you find me a solicitor, an *avocat?*"

"Easily—tonight at supper."

"Thanks, and remember—more rum, less sweet'ner!"

He bowed from the room, and as he closed the door she impishly lifted her mug toward him. Captain 'Lon, when he appeared, better damn well have some answers! What had he got her into? Then she hedged—maybe she would be better off not to know everything. The room was warm, with a coal fire in the grate before September cooled down, and she had not needed that third flip. Elzada had never seen a coal fire. After she napped, she took a taper to the fire and lit her candle. She tidied, arranged her hair, and put on a colorful dress Marie-Paule had made years ago. It had never been worn—a dress like this at Morning River? She hoped Marie-Paule knew, somewhere, that her pretty dress was taking supper tonight in Boston.

12

When she came from her room to descend for supper, Elzada heard men's voices from the dining room. One said, "This is good, Rufus—what did you call it?" When Rufus answered, she knew she had a friend—as when two boys steal apples together. He said, "I thought you'd like it. That's flip. My secret formula."

The three men stood when Elzada came, and Rufus stepped forward with, "Good evening, Miss Knight. May I present Mr. Blake, Mr. Dunbar, and Mr. Shreve?" She held her hand first to Mr. Blake, saying, "My mother's first husband was a Blake—an Indian brained him with a tomahawk." She saw that she had selected a good starter. She noticed, too, that the three men were all younger than she, and that they were admiring. She was flattered. So far, Boston was all right. "Soon after that she married my father."

Rufus held a chair at another table, and Elzada sat. She caught his eye sidewise, winked, and said, "Tea?" To the men she went on, "My mother was a Townes. Last we knew she had a brother with a business in Salem."

"John Townes?"

"Yes—a younger brother."

If getting brained by an Indian hadn't been a good opener, Elzada scored with John Townes. Rufus leaped into the matter: "Miss Knight is down from The Maine on business—she came this morning on the *Madrigal*." But Mr. Blake returned to the subject.

"Niece of John Townes, eh? I'm afraid your uncle won't speak too well of me. I practice law, and I've had to sue him now and then. Always settles in time, but makes me wait. I'm told Townes is well thought of in Salem, but here in Boston—no. He has interests here, too, you know."

"I didn't know that."

"Indian, you say! This from Shreve. "If something isn't done, and soon, about those savages, we'll all be burned alive in our beds. Every day, news of more atrocities. I don't understand how you people can live at The Maine, in constant fear of your lives!"

"I have heard of some disturbances," she began. "But I live pretty far down, and I'm not at a settlement. We've had no problems. Fact is, I've never seen but one Indian in my life, and he was a long-time friend of the family. A Micmac, he made canoes for the *coureurs de bois*." She tossed off the French to needle Rufus, and noticed that he ignored it. "The *coureurs de bois* are French adventurers trading into Canada." Rufus said that was certainly a good thing to know.

"Well, we hear that things are far from serene, all along York and Lincoln." This from Mr. Dunbar, and Elzada thought it was because he felt it was his turn to say something.

Elzada tried her spurious tea and told Rufus it was superb. He offered fowl and lamb, and she chose the lamb. A bit of fish first, and everything followed by a dessert of meal and plums. Very tasty. Rufus did set a good table. When the men rose to go they said good-night, and Elzada spoke to Blake. "I need a solicitor— could I have some of your time?"

"Certainly." He turned to Rufus and asked if the dining room would be available tomorrow afternoon for a conference.

"Of course," said Rufus. "About tea time?"

Rufus barred the door when the men left, and from the stairway Elzada said, "Goodnight, Mr. Achorn." He came over, and barely audible, he whispered, "Bonne nuit! Dorme bien!"

She whispered back, "À demain!"

Her fire had been attended and her candle lit. She opened a shutter, but Boston was dark. She made ready for bed, and under the covers she started to say, "The moon is down . . . " but she never finished. Instead, she thought, "What's wrong with Uncle John?"

Asleep, she heard movement and rose to one elbow to see Rufus kicking her door open to bring in a break-fast tray. "Good morning—it's neither early nor late, but time to eat."

"I never had breakfast in bed in my life!"

"It makes an excuse to have a talk. Captain Plaice said I was to give you every care and I don't intend to offend Captain Plaice. Please, don't be modest—sit up and eat while the cakes are hot. I'm an innkeeper, and have seen ladies in bed many times. And I have a question."

Elzada arranged her pillow and began to eat. She drew her nightgown together at her throat. Rufus brought a chair, sat by her bed, and asked, "Do you know a Mr. Reginald Flanders?" He was watching her intently for any reaction.

"No." There was no reaction.

"A big man; a huge man. Long brown hair and the face of a pirate—cruel, ugly. You don't know him?"

"No."

"Then why does he want to see you?"

"Now look, Mr. Achorn—Rufus—what's this all about?"

"I'm asking you. Captain Plaice gave me strict orders to keep you safe and out of trouble, and I'm leery of this Flanders. He came this morning before it was hardly light, asking for you. How does he know you? How did he know you're here? What does he want? How does he know your name?"

Elzada used her napkin. "That was good!" she said. "Now, I have no idea who this man is, but he's got to be here with the knowledge of Captain Plaice, hasn't he? Who else knows I'm here? Just you, and the three men last night."

"If you say, but I don't like his looks. He wouldn't tell me what he wants. Said when you're ready to set a bucket on the front steps, and he'd come within the hour."

"All right. Rufus, you don't know why I'm in Boston—the young men of last night don't know. Only Captain Alonzo Plaice. And he must have sent your Flanders. I'll see him, but not until I've talked to Lawyer Blake."

13

"You haven't really given me anything to do," Lawyer
Blake was saying. "There's no problem about drawing
agreements, but first we need somebody to agree with.
I can pass the word around, and can arrange for you to
meet people. I suppose there will be offers of marriage!
Why did you never marry?"

"It would make things simple, wouldn't it? Well,
nobody ever proposed—except a scoundrel with a fat
wife and ten children. But, Morning River is far from
everywhere, and young men didn't come that far a-
courting. My mother and father wanted me to go to
school, even England, but I never wanted to leave home.
Until now, I've been away just once in forty years, and
I was ten. So I haven't been exposed and I haven't been
inclined."

"Forty years?"

"I'm forty years old, and that's a point. A husband
should be my age, or even older, and suppose I outlive
him and have this to do all over?"

The lawyer smiled. "If a husband should appear, I'm

sure gossip would say it was never love."

"Gossip isn't important at Morning River. If I marry for love, Mr. Blake, it will be to a married man with ten children—and that's a joke. Disregard it."

"What about your land title?"

"My father's will leaves everything to me. I have—had—three brothers; they are mentioned, whereabouts unknown, and were given nothing. My father's deed was from the Plymouth Company. It was confirmed here in Boston—we took the oath."

"A good many people along The Maine wouldn't do that."

"Why not? My father told them it was pretty hard to live away down The Maine and attend church in Boston."

"By the way, your uncle, John Townes, is a Catholic."

"So that's his trouble! I knew that. My mother was Catholic, married a Puritan, then an Anglican, and I'm quite sure died a happy heathen."

"Give me a description of the property."

"Two dwellings on five hundred acres of alluvial farmland. Waterwheel mill. Barn, sheds, outbuildings, smokehouse. Boatshop and joiner's shop. Wharf and float. Timber. And money—my father left considerable money but I don't know its value. Good part of it's foreign."

"And this is remote?"

"I guess! We're almost to the French. Last night when you were talking about Indian trouble—we haven't had any. I was telling the truth about the Micmac."

"From what we've heard, some people in Boston won't believe that. It's a fact—almost every day we hear of new outbreaks."

"Well, bear in mind, Mr. Blake, that I'm farther from

the Indian troubles than you are. My father used to say there was no law east of Monhegan, and no god beyond the Bagaduce. Talking about going to church in Boston—the nearest church to me is Roman Catholic, and the sermon is in French."

After a pause, Elzada said, "I'm going to see Mr. Flanders tomorrow morning."

It was tricky, and it gained her nothing. Mr. Blake clearly did not know Mr. Flanders.

"Who's he?"

So, it would have to be Captain 'Lon.

The next morning, Elzada walked to the wharf, and the *Madrigal* was gone. So no 'Lon now to give her some answers. Tied up was a vessel Elzada seemed to recognize, and as she walked to its stern she read:

WANDERER
Pemaquid

The *Wanderer* had been to Morning River now and then for repairs, and had occasionally brought things ordered through Manny. Elzada remembered she'd lost a mast once in a line storm. Skipper was a peppery old Scot with a beard like a brush fire. She couldn't come up with his name. He'd had some banter with Jules Marcoux as to why a man's beard is feminine in French. *La barbe.* What's ladylike about a man's whiskers? He'd given Elzada a walrus tusk one time; it was on the shelf at home now. She didn't see him aboard, and as she turned away she bumped into him.

"I knew you were here. Fellow runs your tavern was down early asking questions. What gives with asking questions? Soon as he left, down comes a soldier, wants to know why he is asking me questions! Why are they asking me questions? Are you in some trouble?"

"No, no. My father and mother and the Marcoux have died, and I'm all alone at home. I came here on business. Captain?"

He heard the question mark and answered, "Ross."

"Captain Ross. When did the *Madrigal* sail?"

"Funny you asked me that. They asked me that, too. When *did* the *Madrigal* sail, and why is everybody asking? What's it to you?"

"Well, it's no mystery. I came up on her and was hoping to go back on her. Captain Plaice sort of sailed on me and didn't say goodbye. Could you accommodate me back to Morning River?"

"Doubt it. I haven't been east of Falmouth for two-three years, not even to Pemaquid. But they said the *Madrigal* was Islands bound—she'll be right here in about two weeks. If you get stuck . . ."

"Good to know that, thanks."

"I've been known to make exceptions."

"Do you know a Mr. Reginald Flanders?"

"Nope."

"I don't know him, either. He wants to see me. I wonder why?"

"Well, you put it that way, I don't blame anybody for wanting to see you. Maybe he's a mind to ask some more damn' fool questions."

"That might be. Good sailing, Captain Ross!"

"Thank you."

The oyster soufflé was delicious. After she'd eaten, Elzada said to Rufus Achorn, "M'sieur, le seau!"

Simon Aucoin set a bucket on the front steps of the Golden Clarion.

14

"To begin with," said Mr. Flanders, "my name is not Flanders, but for now that is between us."

It had taken him all of five minutes to arrive at the Golden Clarion after the signal pail had been displayed—confirming the suspicion of Rufus Achorn that Flanders or his lookout was not far away. And Rufus had been quite right about the gentleman—he was not a beauty. Rufus had knocked on her door to tell Elzada that Flanders was below, and he had whispered, "I don't like his looks—I'll be handy if there's trouble." But Elzada descended to meet him in the assurance that Captain 'Lon, and only Captain 'Lon, could have arranged for Flanders to call.

He was broad in the shoulders, very broad, and his head seemed small according to. His great wad of rope-brown hair had been shaped into something of a comical coif by the tight seaman's cap he now held in his hand. His ears stood from under the thatch like ringtails on a schooner—side canvas to catch extra wind. His nose, something of a cucumber, stood high under his

squinty eyes because of the length of his lantern jaw. It
went down and down and down. Mr. Flanders would
be called an "orignal" by Jules Marcoux—a moose. "And
in the second place," he added, "I am aware of my
appearance and beg you to accept it at face value." He
smiled, or seemed to, by turning his jaw askew in a way
that gave him a bit of trouble in bringing it back. "Behind
all this . . ." he gestured at his nose, " . . . beats an
honest heart and we will become good friends. I know
why you are in Boston."

"Captain Plaice?"

"*Captain?* Yes, Captain Plaice. I have his letter to you—
please read it."

Ceremoniously he held a chair, she sat at a table, and
he handed her the letter:

> Elzada, Love—Mr. Flanders is to be trusted and
> can help you. In two or three weeks I'll see you
> again—if not in Boston, at The Maine. Lon.

"I've never seen handwriting by Captain Plaice and I
can't judge if this is his."

Flanders said, "He told me you'd be careful about
that, so he gave me a sort of countersign. If you doubt
that letter, I'm to say something only you and he will
understand."

"As?"

" 'The ends of the earth and a wife and ten children.' "

Rufus had been hovering about the kitchen door, so
now Elzada turned to call to him, "Mr. Achorn—might
we have flip?"

"Flip?" said Flanders when Rufus brought the mugs.

"Yes, sir—flip. My specialty; a down-Maine secret. Miss Knight taught me to make it."

To clear everything up for Rufus, Elzada said, "Mr. Flanders and I will talk privately. Captain Plaice has sent him."

"Certainly—thank you!"

Flanders spoke in a low voice, and quickly: "I'll send you a young man to help you on your land. He's married and has two small sons. He's a boatwright, and he'll be glad for your shop. He's somewhere in his middle twenties. You see, Leftenant—that is, *Captain*—Plaice has told me your story, and I've been able to act on it. The fellow will want to visit your place before he agrees to anything, and that should be soon. What else do we need to say now?"

"Well, what about this *leftenant?*"

"Perhaps I shouldn't have said that. But in time we'll have no secrets—Your *Captain* Plaice had a brief time in His Majesty's Navy. You didn't know that?"

"No."

"He was young—it was before he came to America."

"But old enough for a wife and ten children?"

"Means nothing to me. Your captain seems still a young man. He spoke as if you might be his betrothed?"

"I don't know his age. I suppose he's fifty. I was in my teens when he first came to Morning River for boat work. Ever since then we've joshed about a sailboat romance. He brought me to Boston, but we've had no romance. Where is he now?"

"South. The Islands. I'll see him in two weeks, but perhaps not here in Boston. Shall I tell him your problem has been solved?"

"Has it?"

"I think so. Formalities, is all. You call this flip?"

"Flip it is. Your first?"

"My first. It likes me."

"Then you'll enjoy your first visit to The Maine. We've always been flip people."

"Pure Socratic reasoning!" He held his mug aloft. "I'll visit The Maine soon if just for the flip! But, thanks to you I'll have more reason than that. No, I've never been to The Maine. How far is your place from Monhegan Island?"

Something of a question, thought Elzada. What might it reveal? Why Monhegan? Distance from Monhegan, she thought, would be a reasonable part of the description of any place along The Maine. "I'm curious as to why you ask me that," she said.

"Because I want to know."

"All right—fair enough. But I don't rightly know. Distance along The Maine is a matter of time, not miles. Less than half a day with the right wind; pick the wrong day and that's too bad. I was never the sailor in our family. Thing to do is wait on the wind."

"How about the Bagaduce?"

"Same thing. It's in the other direction. I've never been to the east'ard. Why the Bagaduce?"

"Same reason—I want to know. I'm coming to The Maine to find these things out for myself—but not until you're home and can show me hospitality. Flip and hospitality. Probably the summer's best?"

"Next summer? Please come. Don't you have Smith's map?"

"I do, but not with me. I've memorized it. Do you think Smith's map shows The Maine as it is?"

"My father always believed so, but it shows cities that never existed, and the wrong names for some that do. My father always laughed that Smith shows Boston up in Yorkshire."

"Yes, he does. And that's where this young man lives. It's Georgeana today. Fellow's name is Norman Kincaid. Boys are four and not quite two. Good, smart, young man, and a fine wife. A-Number-One all the way. Do you need a lawyer?"

"I have one, here. Mr. Achorn introduced us. Name of Blake."

"I don't know him. I'll check him out. We ought to have a memorandum of your proposition, something for Kincaid to go by, and the agreement to come later. Now, Miss Knight—very important; nobody is about to abuse you and nobody is about to try. I have my reasons for coming to see you, and some day you'll know what they were. When you need me, set out the bucket."

Elzada took the last of her flip, smiled, and felt obliged to offer her thought, "Well, I'm delighted to have everything settled!"

Flanders, or whatever his name was, saw no humor in this—or seemed not to—and said, "So am I." He stood up to go.

Elzada gave him her hand, and he bowed ceremoniously with one leg stuck out in a manner Jules Marcoux used to affect with his Marie-Paule when he was playing the great gentleman. Jules said it was the way to pay respects to a lady. "Your name? she said.

"Of course. In Boston, I am Reginald Flanders, commission agent for West Indian goods, and I must remain so." He leaned to whisper the rest, "My name is James Mavryck—M–A–V–R–Y–C–K. At your service. I am trusting you; you will come to know me well, and we will be friends." He raised his voice then, and said, "Au 'voir!" He left.

Rufus Achorn was in the door to the kitchen, and he looked baffled. So much so that Elzada wondered about that "Au 'voir."

15

King Philip's war, like all wars, was an exercise in stupidity. It will be recalled that when the Pilgrim Fathers were safely ashore at Plymouth, Squanto, the Indian, stepped from the puckerbursh with hand aloft in a gesture of peace and said, "Welcome, Englishmen!" According to the unreliable suppositions of the incompetent historians, the Pilgrims were astonished that a savage child of the wilderness would know any English, so as curiousity tempered their surprise Squanto became a fast friend. This is hogwash. The Pilgrim Fathers knew about Squanto from away back, and would have been waiting for him to appear. He was already legendary. He had, back in 1607, also welcomed the Englishmen who came to settle Popham, up in The Maine.

In 1605, Squanto was one of the five Pemaquid Indians kidnaped by Captain George Weymouth and taken to England. It is not true, as the historians say, that these Indians were to be exhibited as freaks or to be sold into slavery. They were taken back to England so the officials of the Plymouth Company might learn from them about the region intended for settlement. Gorges wrote, "The capture of these Indians must be acknowledged the means under God of putting on foot and giving life to all our plantations." They were never abused, and as soon as they calmed down after being kidnaped, they were tractable enough. Three of them lived in England with Gorges; two with Lord Chief Justice Sir John Popham. That's not the poor part of town. From the beginning, it was meant they should return to their homeland. Squanto came back in 1606. Another, Nahanada, was in Bristol while Jabez Knight was apprentice there to Boatwright Warren Quintaille. He was conspicuous in his stylish European clothes—made to his measurements by Sir John's London tailor. Squanto and Nahanada learned to speak English in England.

No doubt somebody on the wharf, as the *Mayflower* sailed, called to Elder Brewster, ". . . and if you run into Squanto, give him my regards!" From his wigwam at Pemaquid Point Squanto sallied whenever he heard of new arrivals from England. He went as far east as Newfoundland, and we know he went to Massachusetts. Oh, yes—at Saint Saviour on Mount Desert Island, the Jesuit missionary Massé taught Squanto to speak French. Many Maine Indians were reasonably trilingual.

It was because of Anglophile Squanto that Massasoit of the Wampanoags took up with the Pilgrims, embraced their piety, and said that when he died he hoped to go to the White Man's heaven. (Elder Brewster spoke a good word for him, and he did.) Massasoit also gave his two sons English names, so Wamsuta became Alexander and Pometacom become Philip. (Alexander and Philip were two early Saxon rulers of Macedonia.) Massasoit made a peace treaty with the Pilgrims in 1621, and lived by it

scrupulously until his death in 1660. After his death his
first son, Alexander, held to the treaty, but English-
Indian relations had begun to sour and he was hard put
at times to keep his warriors quiet. Things were in bad
shape by the time Philip took over, and it wasn't long
before he had organized the tribes and was making ready.
King Philip had some 10,000 warriors ready to whoop.

The Indians were far from all wrong. The Pilgrims
were fairly decent people and Squanto and Massasoit
liked them. But up along The Maine, the people were
of a different stripe. We read of them:

> The state of society was distinguished by its
> lawlessness. Every man followed his own impulses
> unchecked. The grossest immoralities prevailed.
> The Indians were cheated and outraged in every
> way to which avarice, appetite, or passion could
> incite depraved hearts. There was no sabbath here;
> no clergy to proclaim the gospel of Jesus Christ,
> with its alluring promises and its fearful retribu-
> tions. Some royal commissioners were sent out to
> investigate affairs. Their report was appalling.

So the Plymouth Company, back in England, learning
the kind of people their colonizing efforts had spon-
sored, took steps. Governor Robert Gorges, Admiral
Francis West, and the Reverend William Merrill—Merrill was Episcopalian—had full authority to clean up The
Maine and make decent people of the Mainers. Parson
Merrill approached his mission with zeal, but was not
well received along The Maine. He found his job hope-
less, quit, and returned to England in disgust.

Those early Mainers, so wicked, were scattered
between Casco Bay and the Penobscot River. Mostly

around Sheepscot Bay, and on the islands. This was the
Gorges land, and fisheries brought the people. To the
west'ard, Falmouth to the Massachusetts lands, settlers
came from Massachusetts and at later times. They may
have been a better class of people. But they were crude
in their relations with the Indians and kept the matter
of land titles at a boil for a long time.

Of the six sources of land titles in Maine, the first two
are "possession" and "Indian deeds." The third is the
French patent of 1603, and then the several English
charters and grants. Jabez Knight, at Morning River,
had certainly been safe with "possession." His French
deed was spurious, and he knew it. His English deed,
stemming from charter of James I, and later confirmed
by Massachusetts, would stand up for what it was, but
his part of The Maine was also claimed by the French
and the Dutch, and may or may not have been a reasonable part of the Plymouth Company grant. French,
English, Dutch—take your pick, but Jabez was certainly never worried about any Indians.

The squabble over lands between English and Indians was mostly a matter of definitions. Indians and Indian
tribes never owned any land—it was merely used.
Everybody used it. So when an Indian, or a chief, felt
kindly disposed towards a good friend who had given
him a bauble, or made him a flip, he would sign over
the rights to shoot rabbits, dig clams, cut wood—he had
no notion he was "conveying," and he never meant the
Englishman should put up a fence and order him off.
Go into the Registry of Deeds in the York County court
house at Alfred, where Maine's oldest records are kept,
and read between the lines of some of those "Indian
deeds." They smack of Anglo-Saxon chicanery, duplic-
ity, and equivocation—the Indian was indeed abused.

Being robbed of tribal lands is bad medicine, and the Indian finally boiled over.

But nobody ever organized the tribes against the French the way King Philip did against the English. The French treated the Indian well, verily like a brother. The Indian had his tribal ceremonies, and was accordingly susceptible to the rituals of the Roman Church. Every French migration brought its Jesuit priest, and French and Indian sat down together at Mass. The French never denied the Indian, as did the English at Boston, his gun, powder, balls, knife, and—his rum. The Indian had long since given up his bow for hunting, and it was a matter of food when the Bostons made a law to take all muskets away from all Indians. Massachusetts sent militia up along The Maine to enforce this.

The way the French fraternized with *les sauvages* had one most interesting result. The king of France was open-minded enough to realize that the overnight weddings of tepee hospitality were casual enough to be excused, but the way his colonists were marrying up permanently with the young squaws made him wonder about the future motherhood of New France. Thus came the *filles du roi*, or the young ladies of the king:

> Les premiers colons qui vinrent s'établir dans la Nouvelle-France étaient célibataires . . . les jeunes filles étaient rares dans la colonie. C'est alors que le gouvernement du roi se décida à envoyer dans sa colonie de la Nouvelle-France des jeunes filles qu'il destinait comme épouses aux jeunes colons.

This took some burden off the Indian maids, and it also emptied the orphanages of France. Assuring us the girls were all virtuous, the historian adds that because most of them were city girls and unready for the severities of life on Canadian farms, the wholesale matings were not entirely successful. At the Church of the Incarnation, thirty couples were married at one Mass. But this does show that the French approached their colonial problems with some thought—it is not easy to imagine Oliver Cromwell shipping wenches to the staid Puritans of Boston.

By the time Massasoit was about to go to the White Man's heaven, the accumulation of the White Man's faulty Indian policies had well soured the relations. Massachusetts had come to be recognized as the proper protectress of The Maine, but wasn't doing much to help. The militia sent made some mistakes—as with the papoose of Chief Squando. Squando (not our old friend Squanto) had been a friendly Indian, living peacefully with the English at The Saco, and he was quickly turned to a bitter enemy by English stupidity. Some of the militia sent to deal with the Indians and promote harmony were lunching one day on the bank of the Saco River, and they saw a canoe coming along the shore, paddled by a squaw accompanied by a child. A baby. Now, an Englishman named Jocylyn had written a book about his summertime visit to America, and in it he said, "The Indians can swim naturally, striking their paws under their throats like a dog, and not spreading their arms as we do." These foolish soldiers thought now was a fine time to find out, so they tipped over the canoe to see if the baby could swim naturally. Jocylyn, it appears, was wrong. Squando was not happy about the murder of his child, and spent the rest of his life hating the English.

So Massachusetts was sort of setting The Maine up for trouble. The settlements in The Maine numbered about a dozen, but were scattered, and many settlers didn't live by the villages. The incident of the Squando baby gave King Philip something to wave around, and he did. The trouble began. A trial sally was made on Thomas Purchase, just below the falls at Brunswick, on the Androscoggin River. He is on record as a "sharp trader," which means he cheated Indians, so on a pleasant day in September of 1675, twenty Indians came howling out of the forest to invade the honorable gentleman's home. Good thing for him he wasn't home. The Indians stayed around, scaring the women, stealing things, and long enough to cook a sheep and eat it. They had been hoping to have some fun with Tom, so his absence took the joy out of the occasion. They didn't burn the place, but promised to come back some day and do that. A day or two later some Indians, maybe the same ones, tackled old Tom Wakely at Falmouth, now Portland. He lived at a distance from a neighbor, with a household of seven—three of them small children. Over on Casco Neck, George Ingersoll saw smoke where the Wakely home was afire, and the next day went over to investigate. All seven had been killed, their bodies left to burn in the fire, and the three children had had their brains dashed out by tomahawks. Soon after that Ingersoll was attacked, and he lost a son. Then two houses at Saco were attacked, but there had been a warning and no lives were lost. At Scarborough, twenty-seven homes were burned. So it went, and as the Maine communities were being reduced, there was no great help from Boston. What Massachusetts did do was done badly.

One war party of three vessels from Massachusetts took a lacing from the Indians at New Meadows, proving that the English soldiers needed training. Well, the

Indians didn't fight fair. They skulked and sneaked, and hid behind trees so they wouldn't get hurt. A detachment of sixteen soldiers came to handle the Indians at Winter Harbor, now Biddeford Pool. Turned out to be a hundred and fifty Indians, so the English retreated gallantly. Another twelve Englishmen came up to help, walked into the usual ambush, and with one salvo the Indians got all twelve of them. Bloody postscripts to the drowning of Squando's papoose.

In December of 1675, Governor Winslow of Massachusetts thought things had gone far enough, so a thousand soldiers marched on the Narragansett village, and brought King Philip's capers to an end. Taking a tip from that great and illustrious Puritan leader, who slaughtered the innocents at Drogheda, Governor Winslow's men outdid Cromwell by butchering a thousand women and children who happened to be Indians. He did. They got six hundred warriors first, and then they really went to work. One historian said this fury was aroused by the tomahawking of a three-year-old child at Berwick, up in The Maine, but real close to Boston. They caught King Philip soon after that, and cut off his head. Then they sold his wife and child into slavery in the West Indies. That was in 1676, just one hundred years before our Declaration of Independence.

But it was in 1673, while things were building up, that Elzada Knight left the loneliness of her Morning River to go to Boston looking for a "manager." When she told Mr. Blake that she was unaware of mounting Indian tension, he seemed doubtful of that, but she was thinking toward the east'ard—about Passamaquoddies, Micmacs, and Maliseets who would remember Jules Marcoux with respect and affection.

16

At breakfast, Rufus Achorn introduced his new serving girl, saying his dining room had become busy enough to need one—thanks to flip. Charlotte was a bit chubby, pink-cheeked, and well featured, and Elzada guessed at maybe coming up to seventeen years. She ducked a curtsy which Elzada surmised was newly acquired, and she wondered if Rufus had been teaching that in the kitchen. That would be something to see! "She's going to live here," said Rufus, "her folks have had misfortune up on The Maine, and she has no home."

Charlotte drew a breath, choked up, and Rufus hurried on, "Indians. Charlotte is alone."

Elzada had no answer, so just pressed the girl's hands in her own, gaining a response of understanding. "Thank you," said Charlotte, and then came the improbable, "I'm called Chuck!"

That gave Elzada something to answer, so she said, "Chuck it is, then—let's you and me be friends!"

"Yes, ma'am—how would you like your eggs?"

Rufus stood apart to watch and instruct Chuck, and

found chances to round out her story. A raid at The Saco; three homes burned. The Bonython family had been erased except for Chuck, who ran to hide in the woods. When Elzada asked, reasonably enough, how Chuck had come to Boston and how she had found the Golden Clarion, Rufus became evasive and shrugged off an answer. Well! Must be reasons. The Achorn-Aucoin question persisted. Chuck was in the kitchen, so Elzada asked, "Est-ce qu'elle parle français?"

Rufus knew Elzada could test that, so he said, "No. But originally her family was French. A friend of mine knew them."

So, as she ate, "Who knows whom?" How did Captain 'Lon know about Rufus Achorn? How would be Bonythons, at The Saco, have a common friend with Achorn? Why had Achorn been so fussed up when his French was discovered? "I am in no danger in Boston— but *we* must be careful." Why *we*? Why did that Mavryck person toss off an irrelevant *au revoir?* Why had that bothered Achorn? Her wonderment was interrupted.

"It's the flip," Rufus was saying. "The flip brings me customers. I'm in your debt. Tonight Mr. Blake is bringing friends."

"Good—I was going to ask you how to reach him. I have some work for him. Will you see that I have a word with him? And another thing—can you suggest a dressmaker, a sempstress—une couturière—who will make me some clothes?"

The supper hour was indeed busy, and Chuck was amazingly efficient for a first time. If she faltered with a spoon or a plate, she kept the flip mugs filled, and that seemed to please everybody. Lawyer Blake spoke to Elzada as soon as he came in, and they would meet tomorrow, at the inn. At tea time. Elzada ate slowly, assuring Chuck she was in no hurry and to care for the other guests first. It thus happened that she was still eating after others had gone, and she had Chuck to herself. The girl had a lovely smile, clean complexion, and straight and good teeth. Her feet were in shapeless moccasins, suitable enough for open country, but hardly right on a floor. Her homespun gray dress was by no means new, but it was strong cloth and wore its age well. The jacket over her shirt was of leather, but wild or domesticated Elzada couldn't tell—it was the usual jacket with alderwood buttons and loops that most Mainers wore, and they seemingly lasted forever. All this was Saco garb, and not for a barmaid in Boston.

The next morning Chuck brought Miss Selma Beddington upstairs and tapped at Elzada's door. She had come at Mr. Achorn's bidding, and as she stepped into the room Elzada saw the yellow ell-tape hanging from the clasp of her reticule. She looked the part of a sempstress—squinty-eyed, stooped, intent, skinny, lackluster, and not at all stylishly dressed. "May I be of service?" she said.

"Yes, and Chuck—I'd like you to stay."

Elzada stood fingering her chin, wondering what she was about to do, and Miss Beddington looked her over with critical eye. She nodded as the inspection went on—she approved. "Yes," said Miss Beddington to herself, "that is a shape to sew to!" So Miss Beddington was not ready for Elzada's words. She said, "I want you to measure Miss Bonython here and make her some clothes—skirts and shirts to start, and measure her feet so you can find her some boots."

"Her?"

"Yes, her. When I was her age I was far better dressed,

and I lived four-five times as far from Boston. Make her a couple of outfits so she'll be the finest barmaid in Boston, and then something else fit for a party, maybe. Miss Bonython and I are both down from The Maine, and we need some new clothes."

Miss Bonython was in a trance. Miss Beddington hesitated until Elzada said, "Come, come!" Chuck then found words. "But, Miss Knight—I have no money."

Miss Beddington had started towards Chuck with her tape, but at this protestation of poverty, wondering about payment, she turned to look at Elzada. Elzada said, "I happen to know that Miss Beddington doesn't plan to charge you anything."

While Miss Beddington was measuring Chuck, Elzada told her to finish some things for the girl first, and if she didn't get everything done before her home-going, a boat could bring them later. "I'll pay before I go," she said. Chuck had her arms in the air while Miss Beddington encircled her bust, and she said, "Does Mr. Achorn know about this?"

"No. This is between you and me—and Miss Beddington. Why do you ask about him?"

"I can't help wondering. After the Indians, somebody gave me a note to Mr. Achorn, and said to keep going until I found him. He read the note, took me to a room, and here I am. Why? Why was he good to me? Is he going to pay for these clothes?"

"No. Who gave you that note?"

"I don't know. A man I never saw before. He told me Mr. Achorn knew my father, but I never heard of him before."

"Curious. Well, your new clothes are a gift from me, and you owe me nothing. I have nobody to buy clothes for except myself, and I think you need some more than

I do." Miss Beddington turned toward Elzada with the tape and Chuck was told she might leave, " . . . if you wish." She said, "I do wish—I'm going to cry and I'll do that alone."

Miss Beddington was firm-handed, and she came to know Elzada fairly well before she had all her figures— or Elzada's figure—on her slate. Everything settled, she said, "This is something of an order!"

Elzada gave her money, took a receipt, and said she'd wait word for fittings. When Miss Beddington was gone, Elzada leaned against the inside of her door, and although she wasn't crying, there were tears in her eyes.

Miss Beddington had said, "This dress you have on is beautifully made!" Elzada had answered with the inane apology that started with Eve, "I've had it for years!" Then she had told Miss Beddington about Marie-Paule Marcoux—how every stitch of clothes at Morning River Farm had been made from scratch right there, save only what came by boat. She told Miss Beddington about the bale of Chantilly lace and how Marie-Paule, wealthy with Chantilly lace, had even put it on woolen mittens. Miss Beddington had said, "I may not please you—her stitching is beyond what I can do. But there—I may be a bit more up-to-date!"

"Do be! The social program at The Maine is thin, and I may never get to wear what you make me. But, I want to be ready if we ever have a grand ball or . . . "

Miss Beddington looked up at the unfinished sentence.

" . . . or a wedding."

So she leaned against the door a bit longer, wondering about that wedding, and soon she went down to dinner.

17

Rufus seated her gallantly, and Chuck brought the food. Chuck said nothing; kept her eyes averted. The noon meal went on in silence. Then Chuck exploded, threw her arms about Elzada nearly to shove her from her chair, and sobbed. Rufus came from the kitchen to discover this, and wisely turned back to the kitchen. And, without a word, Chuck went to the kitchen. Mr. Blake arrived.

He had a man with him and introduced him as Mr. Daubney Smart, an attorney with much experience on land claims and deeds—he was to assist with Elzada's papers. "Mr. Smart," said Blake, "has been attorney for Mr. John Townes, and even though we've crossed swords, I respect his ability and have asked him to help me." Elzada looked up at Blake's face, but he betrayed nothing as he spoke of John Townes. Elzada realized she was not expected to say anything.

Instead of waiting for Chuck to clear the table, Elzada moved to another table, and the two lawyers sat with her. "First," she said, "we should come to terms. Can you give me some idea of what I'll be expected to pay?"

"You don't know?" said Mr. Blake.

"Don't know what?"

"That our fees have been paid?"

"How would they be paid?"

"Well, I thought you'd sent the money, but I guess you didn't. Whoever did, we've been well paid."

"We've been well overpaid," said Smart.

Blake handed Elzada a note:

This is to cover legal fees for services rendered to Miss Elzada Knight at Golden Clarion. Please to sign receipt in full and return by same messenger.

Best to let it lie for now, thought Elzada. Had to be Mavryck.

"So," said Smart. "What can we do for you?"

"I think I've found my man. Name is Norman Kincaid, from Georgeana in Yorkshire, The Maine, I haven't met him—there's a third person. But he'll come to my place later to look things over. I ought to have a memorandum of agreement, with the follow-up contracts if he and I agree. Right?"

Blake said, "I'd suggest a period of probation."

"Good—five years, ten years? But I expect this is going to be one of those things you do once and are stuck with it. Best to be sure from the beginning."

Smart was nodding in agreement. "Not unusual for parents to make such an arrangement with children, but I never heard of its being done with a stranger."

"I've neither chick nor child, so it has to be a stranger."

"When do you expect to see this, er, this Kincaid?"

"Soon. He has a sponsor, and I suspect it's his sponsor who sent you the money. The fact that you have that money makes me think Kincaid is serious. If he can give me a home and care, I'll be glad to give him my property. I'm sure an agreement of this kind will depend mostly on character, rather than binding words, and it would be foolish to try to write everything down. But, we should meditate carefully on what good character should do."

"I wouldn't want to hurry on this, and I'm sure my brother Smart agrees—how much time can we have?"

"As long as needed. I'm comfortable here under Mr. Achorn's roof, I'm having some dressmaking done, and I don't expect a vessel to take me home right away. I may wait for the *Madrigal*, however long that is."

"Today is Tuesday," said Lawyer Smart. "I'll get registry copies tomorrow and settle in. Does a week sound all right?"

"Longer if you wish."

When the two attorneys rose to go, Smart took Elzada's hand and held it while he said, "May I ask you something personal?" She nodded.

"You attended school?"

She laughed, a little too suddenly, and said, "I was sure you were going to ask me why I don't find a man and marry him! You disappoint me! No, I never went to school."

Smart seemed not to notice the laugh, and didn't respond to the marriage bit. "I'm astonished at your knowledge, judgment, and your bearing. Blake, here, told me you were down from The Maine and wanted legal help, and I expected to find—well, I didn't expect to find a charming, intelligent, educated, and very beautiful woman!"

"Thank you, kind sir."

He bowed over her hand and said, "Not at all." They left.

18

It was the next Tuesday that the boy came with a note—
Miss Beddington was ready for fittings. In the afternoon Elzada and Chuck walked from the Golden Clarion along the waterfront to Grimm Street, which was
but an alley extending back between warehouses from
the long "sugar" wharf. A sign on a warehouse said "John
Townes—Salem & Boston" and nothing more. She must,
thought Elzada, make a curiosity call, if not a courtesy
call, but not today. Chuck was much too eager to come
to Miss Beddington's. The ropewalk and sail loft of
Blaisdell & Son stood just beyond, and in a corner of
this rambling building Miss Beddington had her dressmaking shop, with living quarters in the rear. It was
hardly a smart situation for stylish gowns, but was
understandable with the explanation that Blaisdell & Son
was the holdover name of a chandlery and rigging business that was now owned by Miss Beddington's two
brothers. The arrangement was not altogether charita-
ble on their part; Miss Beddington was often useful in
the making of sails, when the brothers would ask her to
step in and do some stitching that was too fancy for

them to attempt. She was in the sail loft doing just that when Elzada and Chuck tinkled the telltale bell on her shop door. She came with a piece of heavy canvas in her hand which clashed with the ribbons and laces about the room. "Gracious!" she said.

Miss Beddington, having had carte blanche from Elzada as to weaves and fabrics, hoped her choices might please, and they did. She had one serving-girl outfit made for Chuck, and everything else well begun. Elzada looked at the things laid out on tables, hanging, or on forms, and at sight of taffeta petticoats, she was minded of her mother's favorite—when Martha was excited, over-joyed, delighted, she would yelp, "Jesus to Jesus!"

"Jesus to Jesus!" said Elzada.

"Mercy!" said Miss Beddington. "Whatever *is* it?"

"Me? In something like that at Morning River! It's beyond belief! Oh! Everything is lovely." Chuck was overcome; ran her hand over things. "All right, Miss Bonython," said Elzada, "off with them, and let's try these things on!" Miss Beddington helped Chuck, and was saying to Elzada, "At the young lady's age, I expect she'll slim some, so I've made these with reef points."

Chuck wore her new outfit away, her castoffs tied with a string. Elzada's wardrobe would come later. "So many things I wanted and didn't have," Miss Bedding-ton had said. "We'll just have to wait until they come!" She struggled for words, so not to sound critical, but she gave the impression that Boston ladies were con-servative, and she had little chance to do something—well—something, so to speak, "flashy."

As they walked back to the Golden Clarion, Chuck held Elzada with linked arm, and communicated a lov-ing squeeze now and then. "Did you have a beau back at The Saco?"

"Sort of, but not really. I guess he's gone. Nobody

could find him after the raid, and some thought he was carried off. Jimmie Gott. But we hadn't decided."

"So you have nobody?"

"Nobody." But Chuck squeezed Elzada's arm, and Elzada understood.

"I live alone away down beyond Monhegan. I have a beautiful place. Think about it in the next few days, and decide if my home could be your home. And give a good thought to the lack of young men in my life. I never married; was never asked. You're a healthy young lady, and will want to marry. I've said enough—think about it."

That afternoon Lawyer Blake came with the papers, a few blank places here and there as to dates and places, but ready enough for a final agreement between Elzada Knight and Norman Kincaid. He showed her where things would need to be filled in, and where to sign, and explained how everything should come to him at Boston for final perusing and filing. Lawyer Smart had secured the seal of the governor, making her title even more secure in the jurisdiction of Massachusetts. Blake said, "We've tried to think of everything, and I hope we have. It's an unusual arrangement—something may spring a leak, but I believe we're watertight."

"Like a pail?"

"Like a pail."

When Rufus set the pail on the steps, Reginald Flanders appeared before Elzada had finished her flip. As he accepted her gesture and approached her table, he studied Chuck, who was standing in evident recoil at the man's appearance. "Ain't I the ugly old devil!" he threw at Chuck, and she nodded vigorously to confirm it.

"This is Miss Charlotte Bonython, up from The Maine; she's working here at the inn."

"I know about the girl," said Flanders. "Her father has helped me in the past. Fearful tragedy. I had her brought here—that is, I arranged for her to come here. Achorn probably surmises. Be kind to the girl— I'm indebted to her father."

"Would I be making a mistake if I invited her to come and live with me at The Maine?"

"No. I doubt if she knows Kincaid, but her father knew Kincaid's father. I think that would be kind, and you'd find the girl useful. Company, anyway. Now, speaking of Kincaid—are we ready?"

"Ready and willing. Did you pay the lawyers?"

"I paid them altogether too much for what they'll do for you, but you've got two good friends at court because of that, and a word from you would help if *I* need them. I saw Kincaid the other day, and he's ready to go. Wife is, too. Indian troubles have the whole coast skittish and scairt, and when she heard you live away to the east'ard she bought that. Nice family. They're lucky—but so are you. Yes, take the girl along."

Chuck brought his flip, and Flanders jollied her in a way that dismayed more than cheered her. "Miss Knight tells me, young lady, that when I come to The Maine you will have a flip waiting for me?"

"It's all right," Elzada said to Chuck. "Mr. Flanders turns into a Prince Charming after a third flip. He knows all about you and me and Morning Farm, and a lot else he doesn't confide."

"Such as," he said, "that come next Wednesday Captain Alonzo Plaice and the *Madrigal* will set out homeward-bound with you aboard."

"Next Wednesday?"

"Next Wednesday. Can you be ready?"

"I will, but my dressmaker won't. Poor Beddington

never had an order like this before, and she's sent for
materials to come. I'll get what she has finished and have
her send the rest."

"They'll follow, I'll see to it. Beddington, you say?
Did you get something fit for the gracious lady who will
be charming hostess at a big banquet?"

"Meaning?"

"Meaning you. I want you beaming fair and ravish-
ingly divine for the big party when I come to have this
young lady make my flip."

"Mr. Flanders," Elzada said to Chuck, "has a way of
making decisions for people, and he has decided you're
going to The Maine with me."

"I decided that before he did."

"Not quite," he said, and he waggled his jaw in his
version of a smile. "You were still at The Saco that day.
I'll probably see you before you sail. I'll watch for the
signal. And now, Miss Chuck, when I came in I noticed
a bucket on the front steps. I think that's a bit shabby
for a respectable inn with such a delightful abigail. Won't
you fetch it in?"

19

September had moved along, and so far October had been pleasant in Boston. Elzada, as her father had, always called this time of year *Septober*, when you'd wake in the morning to smash ice in the wash bucket, and then sweat all day at your work. She was impatient to be home. Mainers away from Maine are always impatient to be home. To wake in the morning in your own bed, ready to jump out and tackle the day. Boston, to a girl who had never seen a street, was fine, and she had liked first rate. She had walked about and had seen everything to be seen, but had not become acquainted enough to be invited inside a Boston home. From the outside, the Boston homes didn't appeal to her. Her own big house at Morning River would make two of them, and the house of Jules Marcoux was better styled. Except for Rufus and now Charlotte, the two lawyers, the Beddingtons, and this Mavryck named Flanders, she had met nobody. Couldn't say, really, that she'd met the Beddington brothers—they'd looked into the dress shop to see where their sister had gone, and there had been an introduction—but with Chuck standing there with most of her clothes off there had been small attention to Elzada. She hadn't made the effort to visit the office of Uncle John Townes, who would doubtless be in Salem anyway. And, she could tell Captain 'Lon, there had been no Boston Bahstids. But she did have the assurance Norman Kincaid would appear, she did have the papers ready, and she was ready to go home. It would be foliage time, and the sugar-maple grove up the slope beyond the curve of Morning River would be at its fiery best if Captain 'Lon would sail on Wednesday.

The morning was warm, and Elzada had her door open into the corridor. She heard the inn door open, and footsteps. Then Chuck's voice, "Welcome to the Golden Clarion!"

In was one of the crew boys from the *Madrigal.* "Captain Plaice sends to ask if Elzada is all right."

Then Chuck: "Tell Captain Plaice that *Miss Knight* is tip-top and dandy, and expects him at once!"

Good for Chuck! She had "moved right in," as the saying went along The Maine, "and took right over." Now that she would live at Morning River, she had become pleasantly possessive, and Elzada was amused with this new relationship. Rufus, having felt obliged to aid Miss Bonython in consequence of the note she brought, was just as well pleased to be relieved of the responsibility. He hadn't wholly figured out why she had been sent to him, although he had "some idea," and Elzada didn't tell him that Flanders had explained to her. Flanders had also made it known that Achorn, a Frenchman, was operating an inn in Boston for some reason besides his health, and that at some time she would understand. Curious, though, that Flanders knew about him, and he didn't know about Flanders. Elzada, who often found her father's remarks quotable, remembered he liked the word *chicanery*. Chicanery.

Rufus had been out about his marketing, and as he came in he called to Chuck, "Captain Plaice is here—please to tell Miss Knight."

"I heard!" Elzada called down, and when she reached the foot of the stairs, Captain 'Lon came in. He came, and did exactly what he had done that last morning at the Morning River wharf—he held his heavy seaman's hands gently over the curves of her hips, so she was neither far nor close, and with a pressure that was neither heavy nor light. He looked at her without a word, and she said nothing. Then to Elzada's intense delight, he lifted one hand, traced her armpit with one finger, and permitted that finger to caress her considerably more than it had, so long ago, in her teens at Morning River. Neither had yet spoken. Neither was aware that Chuck Bonython, eyes bugged and mouth agape, was rather much between them, barely to one side, and was dumbfounded as to why these two ninnies didn't go for each other the way it was perfectly clear they both wanted to.

Chuck's voice penetrated: "What's the matter with you two?"

"Oh! 'Lon, this is Chuck!"

"I'm half inclined to believe you."

Chuck made them breakfast, and Captain 'Lon had said, "We can make do. It's still warm enough so the boys can sleep on deck. Give us a breeze and we'll be home before the *Madrigal* gets crowded. There's only one stop I must make—the others can wait. Strawberry Banke."

"I was there once, when I was a child. My father and mother met there and when I was ten we all went back on the *Elzada*—the sloop I was named after."

When Chuck was in the kitchen, Elzada reached across to take 'Lon's hands, and he let her draw them towards her. " 'Lon," she said, "I won't say I've been worried, but I have every right to be curious. There's so much you need to tell me. What goes on?"

He folded his fingers around hers. "I'll tell you everything in time—some of it needs the right place. I sent you here to the Golden Clarion because I knew something of this Achorn's background—and because Jim Mavryck knows about Achorn and would know where to find you. I found Mavryck, he found you, and you've got your choreboy."

"Yes, but that's far from a mystery. Mavryck knew about Kincaid, he knew about the Bonythons, and goddammit, 'Lon, he knew about *you!* He comes and goes like a Turkish spy. Did you know he paid the lawyers for me?"

"No, but if he did he had a reason. Jim Mavryck is a man of much knowledge and many connections. For now, let's leave it that he is working on something. I suspect, but don't know everything. Expense doesn't worry him. And, he's to be trusted all the way. He and I were friends as boys, before I came to America."

"He didn't know about your wife and ten children."

She thought his expression changed at that. He squeezed her fingers, and said, "Elzada—the time has come to clear that up once and for all. My wife has died."

They sat for some time holding hands, saying nothing, and were unaware that Chuck had approached and was watching with the respect she would accord two bluebirds flitting in the apple blossoms. When Chuck spoke, she said, "Flip?"

"Oh, Chuck," said Elzada, coming to. "What did you do with that bucket?"

"It's in the broom corner, back shed."

"It should be on the front steps—didn't you know?"

"Mr. Flanders said I'm too pretty to have a pail on my piazza."

"Mr. Flanders talks in riddles. Set it out, and in a few minutes Mr. Flanders will come to tell you to take it in again."

So Mavryck learned that Captain Plaice would carry Elzada and Chuck down east, that she would wait for Norman Kincaid to come. He promised to see that the pretty things from Selma Beddington were delivered, and said that in April, without fail, he would come to Morning River Farm. He hoped Elzada would be happy with young Kincaid, and that Miss Bonython would be ready with flip. He turned to Captain 'Lon: "And you, Leftenant Plaice, shall I expect to see you there?"

'Lon grinned. "I'm trying to change my mind about having a garden, and I think I might get used to calling a girl Chuck, but I wouldn't have any idea what to do with Elzada."

Elzada said, "Well, Jesus to Jesus!"

20

Riddle or not, whatever was afoot brought a squad of soldiers to the wharf early Wednesday morning to shake down the *Madrigal*. Elzada and Chuck, with boxes and chest, were about to go aboard when marching boots came to ear. Captain 'Lon was checking water casks on deck, and looked up with, "I thought so!" The pink-cheeked boy in command was pleasant enough, even apologetic. "Oi 'ave, sor, a warrant if needed, but h'only a routine inspection, sor, 'arbor master's h'orders, King's business, h'if Oi 'ave permission to come aboard?"

"Certainly, certainly. Business here is to pick up two passengers to The Maine. No cargo on or off. West Indian goods, Bridgetown to Strawberry Banke and Razor Islands. Feel free. Welcome aboard." Captain 'Lon saluted, and it was evident the young officer recognized the snap of His Majesty's Navy. "Aye," he said.

"Oh," said Captain 'Lon, "there is one thing came aboard here—that butt and the spar. Meant to get it last trip and forgot. Going to be a mail barrel on Outer Razor Island. Chain to moor it's in the hold. That's everything."

The soldiers were not looking for letter boxes. Elzada wondered, as she watched them, if they were looking for anything in particular, or were they just looking on suspicion? They thoroughly checked the cabin and hold, and went over Captain 'Lon's manifest.

"All shipshape?" asked Captain 'Lon.

"Thank you, sor—you're free to go."

"Thank *you*. A cognac from the companion?"

"Not in duty time, sor, perhaps again."

"As you say."

Elzada and Chuck were soon aboard, their effects stowed, and the *Madrigal* was away from the wharf and "filled to the no'th." Captain 'Lon had the tiller, and Elzada stood beside him. "What's your guess?" she asked.

"Guess? Why guess? Why do you suppose they thought I had Jim Mavryck aboard? Funny he changed his mind about coming with us, isn't it? Doesn't his name ring a bell?"

"No. Should it?"

"Just about everywhere except at Morning River, I suppose. He was one of the King's commissioners to manage New York after the Dutch. Footsie-footsie with the duke of York. He's a brother to Sam Maverick in Boston. Mean anything now?"

"Not much. My father used to tell about the damn' mavericks. Contrary people, the odd ones, hard to get along with. Seems to me he felt he was a maverick, being Episcopalian."

"Kye-reck! Maverick was real High Church, and had his differences with the Separatists. He's gone, but this Jim Mavryck is his brother. Changed his spelling back along when he had to deal with the Dutchmen—used to laugh that some of the patroons would give him a Van—Van Mavryck. Smart man, good man, reliable man. I'd hate to have him for an enemy. Well—enough

to say that Boston has some people who would like to
see his pelt on the henhouse door, and my guess is they
thought he was aboard the *Madrigal*." He eyed the trim
of the mainsail.

"It's hard to believe," said Elzada, "that a man who
looks like Jim Mavryck could hide anywhere very long."

"It is not proper for a refined lady of culture and
breeding to cast aspersions on the physical appearance
of her friends." Elzada heard 'Lon's deep laugh as she
turned to confront Jim Mavryck, né Maverick, alias
Flanders. "I've come to answer some of your questions." His jaw wobbled in his smile.

"First, those soldiers *did* find me. You see? Things
are often so simple, and people try to complicate them.
They knew I was here, but arrangements had been made
so they didn't see me when they found me. You've been
most patient. Now, your puzzlement at Rufus Achorn
was no greater than his about you. I reassured him, and
I did it openly in your presence."

"Au revoir?"

"You *did* notice! Good! The *au revoir* meant nothing,
but a little sign with it—Rufus understood. Until then,
he was afraid of you. Thought you were investigating
him, I guess. He was satisfied that you and the Bonython girl came to him by some plan, but he didn't know
what the plan was. Meantime, he was mixed up in other
plans. Enough for now—you'll see our Rufus Achorn
again. At Morning River."

"What about Charlotte?"

"Charity, or, rather, paying a debt. Her father was
at The Saco just as Achorn is at Boston, and just as
you'll be at Morning River. The poor man got Indi-
aned. I had to take care of the girl. I expected you to be
generous."

"You knew I'd ask her to come with me?"

"You did, didn't you?"

"Mr. Flanders," said Elzada, "I'd hate to have you for an enemy."

"So do my enemies." Then, to 'Lon, "Leftenant Plaice, sir, watch for a longboat in the larboard offing—it will take me aboard, and I'll leave you with this sinful creature." He bowed to Elzada, and continued, "Miss Knight, you are involved in a very important negotiation, and some interesting times lie ahead. I'm your friend, never an enemy, and remember that I told you nobody is about to abuse you."

Captain 'Lon had seen the longboat and it was nearing. James Mavryck walked to the Madrigal's rail and stood watching it approach—hands clasped behind his back. He said nothing more, and he didn't look back after he had settled on a thwart of the longboat—to be rowed quietly and briskly toward the shore.

"Go ahead and say it," said 'Lon, and although no sound came, Elzada's lips spoke clearly: "Jesus to Jesus!"

"You heard me explain about the mail barrel we're going to put up on Outer Razor?"

"Yes, and I wondered why my father didn't think of that years ago."

"Funny he didn't. It's not my idea. James Mavryck suggested it. Nice tight butt. Best Eye-talian mountain oak. It's your wedding present."

"*My* wedding present!"

"Aye. Jim Mavryck has a way with decisions. He's made up your mind to marry me. That cask has two dozen place settings of gold-fired Salerno china, made to order, and there's no way to put a price to it. The pottery doesn't make dishes to sell. These were a present to some queen somewhere, but somebody got mad

at somebody else, and the barrel turned up in Haiti. Jim
bought it for you."

"Just one damn' minute," said Elzada, "you mean for
me, or for *us?*"

"Don't wedding presents go to the bride?"

"When there is one."

"All right. But do you know what the tax would be
on that barrel if we'd declared Eye-talian china at Boston? So we have a new mail keg on Outer Razor, and
you can use it to send Jim Mavryck a thank-you."

When 'Lon kissed her, which he did just now, it settled everything for the rest of forever. Elzada awaited
the conclusion of the exercises and said, "Well, it's about
time!"

The afternoon moved along, and while Captain 'Lon
still had both hands on Elzada and none on the tiller,
Chuck interrupted them with the flip. Chuck studied
them with her head atilt, and then, "I'm not really supposed to know about such things, but if you two have
something you'd like to do, I'll steer a while!"

"It's waited; it can wait some more. Chuck, Captain
Plaice and I are to be married."

"I know. Mr. Flanders told me yesterday."

"Don't say it!" said 'Lon, and Elzada didn't.

It was late in the afternoon, a crew boy at the tiller
and Chuck making haddock chowder, that 'Lon and
Elzada sat by the rail forward, facing down east, and
were all-soul-alone. "It was to be to the ends of the earth!
Weren't you supposed to bind and gag me and carry me
away? Now, here we are, and all we're doing is going
home. It's a snide trick to play on the woman who loves
you."

"You haven't loved me, yet."

"Who's had a chance! Oh, 'Lon, I'm afraid for you!

I'm my mother's daughter; she was a real woman all the way, and I've reason to believe she was hotter than a summer skunk. I used to think at times my father hid from her! The day after I first saw you she spent a whole afternoon on the details. You'd made an assault on my girlish charms, giving me pins and needles, and she saw you do it and thought it was high time. I got the whole thing. The glory of it, the wonder of it, the power of it, the beauty of it, the satisfaction of it—and the good-good fun of it. The need for it, the whole thing. I got everything except an actual demonstration. 'Lon, I'm a forty-year-old virgin, I've been saving up, and I want to be everything to you that my mother was to my father."

"You'll do."

"Do! 'Lon, will you cut it out! I know I'll do. My father used to call my mother 'Bunny Rabbit.' She liked that, and would giggle. Well, one day Jules Marcoux and I were up in the swamp at the snares, and we saw a pair of rabbits. Jules laughed, but then he was embarrassed. Then he shrugged, and said, 'But, I guess you're old enough.' I was old enough to know why my father called my mother 'Bunny Rabbit.' "

"I can't imagine," he said, but he held her very close.

21

The crew boys slept in comfort under a sailcloth rigged on the *Madrigal's* tafferel, so Captain 'Lon had his two women below. Elzada was across from him, prim and proper, and Chuck climbed above her. Chuck had taken over the galley chores and was proving an adequate and even innovative seacook. She was below this morning while Elzada stood at 'Lon's elbow by the tiller. Elzada said, "'Lon, you and I have our new toy and we're playing eyeball to eyeball—but pay a little heed to Chuck."

"Oh?"

"Yes—oh. That girl saw her family and friends murdered, probably the boy she wanted to marry, and she's got a big wallop coming up. If the thing hits her with a big bang, it's not going to be a pretty day."

'Lon was nodding. He said, "Funny how fast things can happen. A month ago you needed everything. Now you're an unconsummated bride with an unmarried husband and an orphan daughter to worry-wart." He called below, "Chuck! You offered to steer awhile—come topside for a lesson!"

Chuck took Elzada's place beside Captain 'Lon, and put a hand to the tiller. He showed her how she could feel the movement of boat against water by what the rudder was saying. He showed her how to watch for the flutter along the edge of the mains'l. He had her repeating the names of sheets and stays, learning loo'ard and wind'ard, starboard and larboard, abeam and astern, fore and aft. Chuck's face was a study of rapt attention, her eyes glued to the mains'l. Elzada felt as had Miss Beddington—Chuck could lose a pound or two—girth and heft. The chubbiness would pass, and before long she would be a very pretty young lady. Captain 'Lon was saying, "You see—it's just like everything else in life. It's easy and fun when things go right. Nothing to it. Ride all day and the schooner just about sails herself. But you let things breeze up, and come a cross-chop on a turning tide, and rain-hail-and-snow, and that's when you need a friend. That's when we have to show what we've got. Separates the men from the boys."

"Making a pretty good father!" thought Elzada, and had a pang as she realized Chuck might well be the only child 'Lon would father.

When the trick was over and one of the boys took the helm, Chuck went below and soon called up, "We got haddock chowder enough for a meal left over—shall I heat it or heave it?"

"What else we got?"

"Well, I can heave what's left and make another haddock chowder!"

The pause at Portsmouth was brief. Captain 'Lon brought the *Madrigal* just right for the turn of tide, and she scooted up to the wharf in no time. It seemed to Elzada, although her recollection was dim, that 'Lon tied up just about where her father had brought the *Elzada* so long ago. Strawberry Banke had been Portsmouth now for at least twenty years, but the old name was persisting. "Why," Elzada asked 'Lon, "would anybody in his right mind change a name like Strawberry Banke to a name like Portsmouth?"

"Because we call Charlotte Chuck."

Two pipes of Barbados molasses went ashore, and the *Madrigal* caught the next tide to be whisked down river. In October it gets late earlier and earlier, so the sun was well down at Smuttynose. Captain 'Lon guessed the wind would fade at sunset, and it did. "That's good," he said. "We'll take our time the rest of the way and enjoy things. There's nothing in God's great kingdom to beat a quiet passage down along The Maine—no sea-coast like it any place else. I've come a-whistling down along here in weather you couldn't see a mile, and nobody should ever come to The Maine that way."

The *Madrigal* scarcely heeled all night and did, just about, steer herself. The sun popped from the ocean according to plan, and Captain 'Lon opined the day would offer little wind, but enough to make Halfway Rock, perhaps Seguin. It was so—except for the swells the ocean was calm, and with a merest air the *Madrigal* tenderly eased off one swell to caress the next one. Chuck held the tiller a good part of the time, and Captain 'Lon set her a course that would lie well off Spurwink, but would pass fairly close to Halfway Rock. "From now on," he said, "you're really down east—up to now it's been getting-ready."

Hardly more than a gently swaying baby's cradle, the *Madrigal* moved along. Chuck shouted, "What's *that!*"

"Where away?"

"There—see it?"

Captain 'Lon said, "It's late season for one, but you've spotted a whale, sure enough!"

They watched the whale a long time. He wasn't close, and every time he breached to blow everybody would say, together, "There he is!" They came to Halfway Rock. The crew boys were rigging cod lines at the stern, and Captain 'Lon explained that Halfway Rock drops to bold water and has a haddock hole. To prove him, the boys jerked their arms, and each brought up a haddock. "Good!" said Chuck, "now for a haddock chowder!"

"We'll stay off for the night," Captain 'Lon said, "and won't see Seguin, but we'll have Monhegan Island some time in the morning. And that complicates our schedule. I planned to reach Morning River so we'd have most of the day ahead of us, but the light air has slowed us. Maybe we should pass a night at Monhegan?"

"I've been to Monhegan Island now and then with my father and Jules Marcoux," said Elzada, "but never went ashore. Jules always called it Ile de Nef."

"Used to be Saint George Island to the English; the old Indian name sounded like munhiggin—Indians never spelled anything, so all we can do is come close."

When the *Madrigal* eased in at Monhegan Island, her arrival caused the usual curiosity that began hundreds of years ago and continues today—who is she, where from, who's aboard, what's she want? But Captain Plaice and the *Madrigal* were no strangers to Monhegan—one of the crew boys came from there. Eugene Pitcher—they called him Ginger but nobody knew why. There were two men on the beach, and Ginger waved to them, explaining to Elzada and Chuck, "Uncle Tim and Pooky Sinnett." The men waved back. The harbor wasn't crowded—the carriers of fish were back in England for the winter, so only a few sloops were on moorings. Captain Plaice set the *Madrigal* gently against the wharf and the two men came to secure his lines. "Hi, 'Lon!"

And then, "Kee-rist! He's got two women!"

"Not exactly women, my friends—please to meet my wife and daughter!"

Pretty much stunned at this from Captain Plaice, the men bobbed their heads and showed their disbelief. "It's pretty true," said Elzada. "Maybe you knew my father— Jabez Knight from the east'ard?"

"Him and his Frenchman built my sloop," said the one who turned out to be Pooky Sinnett. "Ten years old and tight's a cup!"

"Thought we might pass the night," said Captain 'Lon. "I'd like to walk the girls up the knoll come morning. Anything you can spare for supper?"

"You short?"

"No—fact is, we're heavy on rum and Holland gin— but otherwise not very ladylike. Something that can't swim would make a great hit. Chuck, here, she's cook."

"Chuck—she?"

"I'm Chuck."

"Chuck," said Captain 'Lon, "is the world's greatest authority on haddock chowder."

"All right, Chuck," said Pooky Sinnett, "if you'll just explain how this reprobate walrus here comes to be husband to the queen of Sheba, and you turn out to be their good-looking daughter, I'll owe you all the goose you can eat."

"No, you don't!" This from Captain 'Lon. "You fetch a goose or two, and come aboard for flip and supper, and I'll tell you myself. But no goose, no news. No flip, either." To Chuck he said, "Can you handle a goose?"

"Geese swim, too," she said.

"Not much around here that don't," said Pooky. "A goose is a Monhegan fish that can fly."

The crew boys went ashore for the night. The two

men knew Morning River and the Razor Islands, and as the events of the evening took shape aboard the *Madrigal* they congratulated "the happy couple." They asked Chuck about growing tendencies and Indian raids "to the west'ard," and although Chuck tightened up she kept her cool. She managed to change the subject: "Actually, except for one thing, this amounts to a wedding party."

"What's the one thing?"

"They ain't married."

"Do tell! Now, that's a crying shame! But I always say, 'First things first,' and anybody that needs a wedding to have a wedding party is real nasty fussy, don't you say so, Tim?"

"My sentiments to a T."

The geese, taken across on Manana Island two days ago, had been dressed and cut, so offered no resistance to Chuck's advances. She had never cooked goose, but knew about ducks, and she performed well—pausing with supper now and then to prove that shipboard flip can manage without milk. Captain Plaice invited the two men to come in the morning with their jugs, as he had "some sauce" he thought was worth their opinions. The men went ashore in good season, and after 'Lon boosted "his daughter" into her berth he stooped to kiss Elzada. "I think tomorrow night," he said, and he went to his bunk.

The next morning the three of them walked slowly up the ancient trail, under the pointed spruces—from tidewater to the crest of the great granite nubble that stands sentinel, landfall of America. Along the way, Chuck had some questions.

"All right, if I'm going to be your daughter, what do I call you?"

Captain 'Lon said, "Lucky."

They settled it. She was to call him 'Lon unless, as might happen, there would be respectful regard for his command, and he would then be Captain 'Lon. As for Elzada, Elzada would be just fine.

"I'm glad for that," said Chuck. "It's a good name. I never heard it before; it sounds as if it has a secret meaning."

"It was the name of my father's sloop."

"Where'd he get it?"

"I have no idea. I thought maybe it was from the Bible, but I couldn't find an Elzada in the Bible."

They came to a sky-blue patch of fringed gentians. Not exactly a carpet, because gentians grow tall. But a wide bed. "I was here once before in the fall," said 'Lon, "and I remember them. Never saw them like this any place else."

"We have them at Morning River," said Elzada, "but never so many. That's the bluest blue you'll ever see."

Chuck said she never saw a fringed gentian before. They, along with everybody else who has ever been there, stood on the crest of Monhegan Island in awed silence. The bright October morning was cloudless, and the ocean was as blue as the sky—both as blue as gentians. Far below, surf was breaking against the rocks, and gulls circled above the spray and the spume, forever at their profession of coastal scavengers. They had been looking seaward a long time before Chuck turned to look toward The Maine and made a long "Oh-h-h!" on an in-drawn breath. The coastline, east to west, was green as the water was blue, and the Penobscot Hills sharp against the sky.

"Now, that's The Maine, and it was from right here that we get the name. When people first came here from Europe, long ago now, they climbed this hill and stood right here. They didn't know too much about where they were, but from here there's no question but you're on an island. So that, from there to there, had to be the mainland."

Captain 'Lon ran an arm about the waist of each of his ladies, drew them to him, and for a while they just looked. Then he said, "That's home to you two. Me, it's a place I found when I was still a boy, and I've never really left it since. I don't plan to." Far away, to the left, a sail showed white against The Maine. It was well loomed in the bright October air. Seemed to be riding out of water.

Chuck broke the spell. "Well," she said, "somebody in this family has to do some thinking. What'll you two pay me for a couple of biscuits apiece and a slab of good goose meat with pepper and salt?"

She opened a basket.

22

Just a few minutes more and the *Madrigal* would round
the ledges and come into the reach behind the Razors.
Elzada stood forward and Chuck came to be with her.
Chuck said, "Do you think I can have my own room?"

"Rooms, we've got. You can have your own, and you
can even pick it out."

"At The Saco, we had one room. Eight of us."

"My room is the big front one over the ocean—used
to be my father's and mother's. The room I had is on
the back, right by the falls. Even with the windows closed
you can hear the water. Maybe you'd like that room."

"Do you think Captain 'Lon will give up the sea?"

"No. Not right away. He can't even stop long this
time—he brought us home instead of going town to town.
He'll go back in a few days—at least as far as Appledore. But the *Madrigal* is an old boat, and maybe he'll
retire when she begins to leak a little. For one thing—
I'd like to go to the Islands with him, at least once. No.
We'll see him when he's with us—but nobody is about
to make a farmer out of Alonzo Plaice. How does it

go?—'every drop of blood pure Stockholm tar.' "

"When do you expect the man to come and do the farming?"

"Before snowfall, I hope. I'm sure you and I could manage through the winter, but I'd rather not."

Elzada put an arm on Chuck's shoulders to draw her close, and with the other hand pointed at the shore line ahead. "Look there, and you'll see the shore open up to a river. That will be Morning River, and as soon as we can see up Morning River, you'll be home!"

It was so, and Chuck looked and drew in another Oh! as the waterfalls and the buildings came around the gooseneck. Captain 'Lon stood with them, and said the tide was right and they could tie up at the wharf for maybe two hours. Then, there was the wharf, and by it a boat. A small boat, but with a house, and the sail down and secured. "Who?" said Elzada.

"Looks-if it's meant to beach out—somebody's been there a time."

It was Norman Kincaid.

He had, as 'Lon surmised, been there a time. He'd explored Morning Farm even back into the maple hills. He came running down from the big house and caught a line from a crew boy. "Where've you been?" he called.

Jim Mavryck had said Kincaid was twenty-two, but there on the wharf in the sunlight he seemed no more than eighteen or so. One might guess he and Chuck were about of an age. His beard was hardly that of grown manhood, and looked as if he'd had great trouble getting it to sprout. He had the inevitable leather jerkin over homespun clothes, and a toque over his sandy hair. His smile was like the sun coming up! He was pleased with the surprise he'd wrought. "Norman Kincaid," he said to Elzada, "and welcome home. I've been waiting three days. And if you don't smell it yet, you will right away—I've got a venison stew going!"

The introductions were made, and Captain 'Lon couldn't resist. About Chuck, he said, "This young lady makes excellent venison stew with fresh haddock."

From first sight, there was no doubt whatever with Elzada. Norman Kincaid was the boy. He had been all over the place and his enthusiasms were evident. The boatshop in particular. His wife and youngsters would be ready when he came for them. The boat below was borrowed but at Georgeana he had a 35-foot sloop he'd built, and it would be coming to Morning River to stay. He had experimented with the mill, and knew how to run it. He knew his wife would love the Marcoux house. Figured it would take two trips to move—one for the family, and then the animals. He had a milking cow and a heifer about to freshen; two ewes and a buck; two shotes; some hens; a pair of pigeons; and two bull calves that would be big enough to work next spring. Yes, he'd looked in the barn and there was plenty of hay.

Captain 'Lon said, "I'm going to the west'ard in a few days—whyn't I pick up the wife and boys, and you can tag along with Noah's ark? Save a trip. I'll have a swept hold."

Well before twilight everything and everybody had settled in. Norman had made his stew at the Marcoux house, so they had supper there. Chuck appeared in her barmaid outfit and gave the meal a formal elegance with a bottle of wine she had found in the cellar at the big house. She prevailed on Norman to toast the bride! Oh, yes—the two crew boys came at Elzada's insistence, although they demurred that socializing of this kind was above their privileges. They had taken the skiff from the boathouse, gone below to anchor the *Madrigal* in deep water, and had come ashore by oar. One of them, after supper, found the violin of Jules Marcoux, tuned it, and played up a storm. Elzada hummed him, and when he got the tune she sang one of Marie-Paule's ancient Provençal songs. The boys returned to the *Madrigal*; Norman took the Acadian canopy that Jules had made for Marie-Paule; Chuck was in her own room listening to the rush of water at the upper falls, and she knelt in the starlight by the window and made her little prayer of thanks.

Captain 'Lon and Elzada had the big front bedroom over the ocean.

23

On the twenty-second of October, 1673, Charles Stuart, by the grace of God king of England, Scotland, France, and Ireland, Defender of the Faith, &c., roused at a movement in his bed and turned to see a bare backside, female, pass through the velour curtains of the royal bedchamber and out of his life forever. She of the bare backside had been noticeably nervous at entertaining her monarch, and Charles had coolly rated her during the attempt as much less than medium in his collection. She was of a similar mind about him, and vastly unsatisfied came from the bedchamber to find Mountleigh, His Majesty's personal procurer, who was waiting to assist her into her clothes, to pay her, and to open a certain door so she might discreetly leave Whitehall Palace unobserved. Mountleigh, when desire encouraged him, often made use of the king's ladies during their departures, and as this young woman appealed to him he dallied at helping her into her clothes. His opinion developed that she was far more competent than the average, and he wrongly concluded that His Majesty had enjoyed a tempestuous frolic with an experienced voluptuary. It was by no means early of the Whitehall morning, but Charles would rest a time yet before being readied for his levee with the ministers. Mountleigh knew there was no need for haste.

On the twenty-second of October, 1673, Elzada Knight, also unclothed, wakened in the big front bedroom of her Morning River home to find herself alone. She had not known when 'Lon left her. The sun streamed at the windows and her just-opened eyes smarted at the brilliance off the ocean. She wrapped herself in her long bed jacket and stepped from her room to go downstairs. In the kitchen, Chuck was at the hearth and warm smells promised a good breakfast. Captain Alonzo Plaice and Norman Kincaid were sitting by a window, and they had just finished cutting the rest of the deer Norman had shot on his first day at Morning Farm. There was, accordingly, a considerable pile of sliced venison ready to be smoked. At supper the night before Chuck had said she knew how to smoke meats, and Elzada was to show her the supply of alderwood, juniper tips, sumac blossoms, and sweetflag stems for firing the smokehouse. Everybody said good morning.

As Elzada went to help Chuck, Captain 'Lon said to Norman, "You think you can haul the *Madrigal?*"

Chuck looked at Elzada and made a knowing and victorious wink. Boats get hauled for repairs—and storage.

Norman said, "I think. She's big for the ways, but we can extend 'em and shore up. We've got lumber on hand for that, and plenty for a cradle. Can do, but . . ."

"But what?" Elzada and 'Lon said it together.

Norman was fishing for words. "Well, I had thoughts during the night. The thing is, Captain Plaice, I didn't expect *you.*"

'Lon reached over and tunked Norman on the chest with a half-closed fist. "Good boy! Been on my mind, too. But you notice I said 'can you haul,' not 'we'—I'm not in this picture. There's a thing called a prenuptial agreement—I'll sign off. Nothing to change your arrangement with Elzada. No claims. And no reason for any—I'm not a poor man. So, how about hauling the *Madrigal*?"

"So it's a prenuptial agreement, eh?" said Chuck. "Then I take it you two are really planning to nuptial?"

Captain 'Lon had reasonably decided there was homework to do. He did make one more voyage to the West Indies that fall, and while he was gone Norman brought his livestock. Norman had given 'Lon a list of seeds to find for next season, and emphasized apple seeds. "Apples, you start with seeds and then graft the shoots," he explained, "and down around Georgeana we can get graftings when we need them." The Kincaids took over the Marcoux house, and Mrs. Kincaid—Nora—and Chuck hit it off like playmates. The two boys were the spirit and image of their father and dogged his heels. Norman's first shop chore was a hutch for the bridal dishes of James Mavryck and it, with the dishes, was in a corner of the kitchen when the *Madrigal* returned. Chuck said it would be indecent to use the beautiful dishes until some people she had in mind got nuptialed. It was Manny, the Portygee, who handled that.

Manny had come over when the *Madrigal* arrived, laying alongside to take care of some boxes and bales, about which there was no public discussion, and then he helped haul the *Madrigal*. Norman had everything ready and the job took no great amount of time. But there had been some joshing about 'Lon and Elzada and their nuptial, so when Manny sailed to the east'ard the next day he had a plan in mind. When he returned, he neatly laid his boat up to the Morning River wharf and assisted a roly-poly character, with considerable swaying, stumbling, and teetering, over the rail and onto the wharf. Norman came from the boatshop to aid in this maneuver, and when Elzada saw this character approaching her house, she thought it was an Eskimo. He wore layers of sealskins, but even so, there was a round, well-set man inside. Manny brought the sealskins into the kitchen and fumbled some of them off before he began his introduction.

Father—the title turned out to be in question—Hermadore had in the beginning faithfully observed the scholastic tenets of the Holy Order of Jesus, and at the height of his zeal had been transported in the company of fifty fishermen of La Rochelle to be their spiritual strength at a place named Port des Gouttes, at Terre-Neuve, or Newfoundland. But as Captain 'Lon found out from Manny, Father Hermadore had been corrupted. Manny had suggested tactfully that a fortune might be made in certain trading and trafficking, with Port des Gouttes in context, and the accursed thirst for gold had persuaded the good priest to forswear his vows and become a trader and trafficker in contraband, with Manny the head contrabander. Elzada got more of the story from the good father himself, in French. His peccadilloes brought Father Hermadore to grips with his conscience, which he was able to handle, but the general of the Society of Jesus was another matter. The general of the Society of Jesus was in Rome, was not familiar with the customs of North America, and Father Hermadore saw no future in journeying to Rome to try to explain. Father Hermadore had accordingly moved in secret from Port des Gouttes to Havre Aubert in les

Îles de la Madeleine, or the Magdalens, which gave him renewed security and made no difference whatever in the affairs of Manny the Portygee. Elzada learned that Father Hermadore did not know if he had ever been excommunicated, but would express no surprise if he should hear so. Manny had prevailed upon the old reprobate to come to Morning River and celebrate a nuptial Mass.

Father Hermadore brought to Elzada's mind the curtal friar of Robin Hood. Hearty, lusty, jolly, booming—such words suited. His sealskins off, he was certainly well fed, and he wore the collar. His double-looped rosary of gold chain and ivory beads fell to an enormous cross of walrus-tusk ivory, and this splendor had no relevancy whatever to the Jesuit vows of poverty. His homespun was heavy and closely woven—he would have to be the best-dressed priest in Acadia. He told Elzada he knew a little Spanish, not much, and he could speak in Portuguese with Manny. Chuck and the Kincaids were awestruck at hearing Elzada converse with Father Hermadore in the rolling *patois d'acadie*; they had not known of her ability. She and Father Hermadore were laughing as they talked, and, again, she thought of Friar Tuck. She quoted:

> The frier he set his fist to his mouth,
> And whuted whutes three . . .

Father Hermadore said he didn't know Friar Tuck. Captain 'Lon asked, "What the hell is a whootie?" Elzada told him he had all winter to get acquainted with the books in the back room.

Manny, delighted at instigating all this, took Norman down to his boat, and they brought back the provisions he had fetched for the occasion. There was a great ham, smoked, crusted with salt, sewn in cloth. A brisket of beef, corned in a small cask. Plovers, smoked Indian-style with the feathers still on. Gaspéreaux and salmon, smoked and strung on sticks. Flour and meal, and a crock of blueberries preserved in honey. And more, and when added to the stores already in the two cellars, quite enough for any wedding feast. Chuck's mentioning a wedding feast caused Father Hermadore's mouth to seep, and he drew a lace-edged linen kerchief from the sleeve of his cassock and decorously wiped his lips.

Miss Selma Beddington of the Boston Beddingtons had not yet forwarded a trousseau, so Elzada had to select from her armoire of Marie-Paule's creations. Chuck was in her Golden Clarion costume, and with eggs and milk from Norman's hens and cow she was once again dealing a true Morning River flip after something of a lack in that department. Elzada descended, magnificent, saying she was ready, and after another flip Father Hermadore arose, belched, dabbed with his kerchief, felt around until he found his walrus-tusk cross, and allowed that he, too, was ready. It was a lovely wedding, and as Father Hermadore proceeded, the bride translated.

Afterwards, Father Hermadore made out a certificate, and Elzada translated it to another piece of paper. Father Hermadore signed both, and so did Norman and Nora and Chuck. Manny shook his head; wasn't everybody in those days who could write his name. Chuck made a pleasantry—she said it wasn't every child that could witness the wedding of her mother and father. Father Hermadore gave his blessing, forgetful that he had already done so. Then, before the feast, Father Hermadore drafted the quittance—Elzada said kittance—that was to deprive Captain 'Lon of any equity in his wife's property. When it was signed and witnessed, he gave the paper to Norman Kincaid. The Eye-talian dishes were used.

Manny sailed the next morning, but Father Herma-dore stayed over one trip to enjoy the Morning River hospitality. He promised to record the wedding, but was evasive about where, and he couldn't even guess at a when. The others might well presume the wedding had been regular, but after a few days of Father Hermadore's bouncing company, Elzada had doubts—which she kept to herself.

The winter was not severe. Norman lofted a sloop and kept busy, with Captain 'Lon on a keg nearby to watch him. Elzada began the instruction of the two Kincaid boys—with Chuck sitting in. In early March the sap started, and 'Lon and Norman, helped by the boys, put buckets on the maple trees. After that, a Maine winter is all downhill.

24

King Charles II appears in this narrative with good reason. He never knew it, but he had much to do with the affairs of Morning River Farm in the year 1674. It is one thing to pick down the books and read what was going on in England and on the Continent in those befuddled days, and quite another thing to figure out why. Reason, as well as kings, was uneasy on the throne. John Milton, who wrote so eloquently against episcopacy, cried out long before there was any Patrick Henry, "Give me the liberty to know, to utter, and to argue freely according to conscience, above all liberties!" But he went on to say that popery could not be tolerated. Everybody wanted the religious freedom to shove his ideas down the other chap's throat, a sentiment transplanted in Boston, where freedom to worship God promoted bigotry. Just before the Restoration, when this Charles II was in exile in Holland, he made his declaration of intent should he be restored to the English throne. By that time England had had quite enough of Butcher Cromwell, the spurious "republic," the joys of

Puritanism, and the military despotism Cromwell had fostered. Comfort in religious matters seemed desirable to many people. But Charles worded it, "No man shall be disquieted or called in question for differences of opinion which do not disturb the peace of the Kingdom." Righto! The poor Quakers, who felt Christ Jesus meant what he said when he said not to swear, refused to swear, and this was clearly against the peace of the Kingdom. The Puritan God, who was always on the side of Oliver Cromwell, gave His opinion that it would be quite proper to murder the Catholic priests at Drogheda, since the peace of the Kingdom was at stake. One historian never cracked a smile and wrote, "The sword is not a good weapon for waging a moral crusade," and then told how Parliament met to vote for religious freedom and soldiers sealed the doorway so the Presbyterian members couldn't get in to vote. The "Test Act" was dandy; it guaranteed that anybody could hold public office so long as he took Communion in the Church of England.

It was about the same all over. James I, the first Stuart king of England, graciously permitted his daughter to marry Frederick, elector of the Palatinate, who was the head of the German Protestant League. This was a sticky thing to be in a sticky place in 1613, when the Thirty Years' War was about to erupt. Bohemian Protestants tackled the Habsburg king, considered bigoted because he was Roman, and then set this Frederick up as Bohemian king. At this, the king of Spain sat up and took notice, because he would be expected to side with the Habsburgs, and England would side with son-in-law Freddie. Spain didn't care to make any more waves in the Channel. Besides, James hoped to marry his son Charles to the Spanish princess, and the king of Spain

could see that might work out just fine. He would
demand that England ease off on badgering Catholics,
and that any children should be brought up as Catholics, thus sewing the throne of England up for you-know-
what. The Spanish princess didn't go for Charles, so
none of this came off, but while the ambassadors were
negotiating, the Palatinate was overrun with Spanish
soldiers. King James I wasn't all that swift.

Over in France, King Louis XIII was willing that his
daughter Henrietta should marry Charles, but with the
same stipulation—lay off the Catholics. James had made
a deal about *them* with Parliament, so he couldn't agree
to that, but he did help in the Palatinate, and finally got
a marriage contract that was well watered down. As
said, he wasn't too speedy. The English and French
thrones went into a cousinship when Charles married
Henrietta, which would lead to later cross-Channel
pleasantries.

James I died in 1625. His son, Charles I, died very
suddenly at Whitehall in 1649—Protector Cromwell had
consulted with His Puritan God, and They had decided
this would be the best thing for all concerned. Came
the Interregnum, the Restoration of Charles II—whom
we lately left asleep in his bed. Since the day James I
had given *Virginia* to the Plymouth Company, things
had been happening in America, too.

The amours of Charles II had been frequent and usually tedious to his doxies. He took a notion to marry a
Spanish princess, too, but once again the idea got side-
tracked. The Spanish king had a daughter, all right, but
he wanted to pass her off on a Habsburg for political
reasons, and Charles was jilted. He turned to his cousin,
Louis XIV of France, who deeply sympathized. Louis
suggested Charles marry Catharine of Braganza, a flower

of old Portugal, because Portugal was in revolt against Spain, and if England would help Portugal, Louis XIV would like that just fine. Charles at that time was having a difficulty with Parliament about a little matter known as "supply," which means dough, and as Parliament continued reluctant Charles was utterly impoverished. So, thanks to Louis XIV, Charles could feather his wallet without waiting on Parliament. A whopping good dowry. Charles pocketed the moolah, sent some soldiers to help the Porties, and took Catharine of Braganza to his bed and well-buffeted mattress. This made Louis XIV happy, and as he was the best-seated and best-heeled monarch of the time, he was able now and then to help Charles, this way and that, and the game went on.

There had been a brush lately with the Dutch. It flared again in 1654. France and Spain were interested, but deemed it wise to show restraint, and left the fracas pretty much an Anglo-Dutch encounter. Charles was a boat buff, and he sent some vessels to seize New Amsterdam in the New World. This came off delightfully; the Dutch offered no resistance. In settlement of this tilt, the English gave up some spice bushes in the Far East, but kept New Amsterdam, which was renamed New York. There was a reason for that.

King Charles II had a brother who was to succeed him as James II. But at the time of the New Amsterdam heist, James was duke of York, with a good settlement, and held the position of Lord High Admiral. Because of the tightwads in Parliament, Charles was forever needing money, so he named his brother James governor of the New Amsterdam properties, with the understanding that he was to make things profitable and relieve the throne of its dependence on Parliament. The duke of York then sent his board of governors to America to put all this into effect—Messrs. R. Nicol, George Carwricks (sometimes Cartwright), B. Cheyney, and James Mavryck. As we know, this James Mavryck was a younger brother of the late Samuel Maverick, an early Nonconformist settler in the Boston area. In addition to managing the lands taken from the Dutch, now called New York, these gentlemen were instructed to find ways to bring Providence, Massachusetts, Plymouth, and The Maine into one congenial colony, working in harmony to make money for His Majesty.

One day the duke of York, studying maps and charts of the area and perusing various grants and patents, decided that the records showed no definite disposition of the country between the Saint Croix River and Pemaquid. Since Louis XIV of France, an excellent good friend of King Charles II of England, had always presumed that Acadia belonged to him, it was perhaps unkind of the duke of York to instruct his agents to pick up this down-east parcel and add it to the rest of the proposed colony. To answer a number of questions— James Mavryck was already busied with the manipulations and maneuvers when first we met him at the Golden Clarion in Boston. To be sure, King Charles II didn't know about much of this, but he had started the ball rolling, and his brother was in charge. The folks at Morning River Farm didn't know about it either, even though Morning River lies between the Saint Croix River and Pemaquid. It was James Mavryck who knew all this, and because he knew it he arrived at Morning River early in the morning of May 23, 1674. The warship that brought him anchored over toward Long Razor Island.

25

Nobody saw the vessel until she was well in past the Razors, and then because she spoke from a signal gun by her stern. This brought Norman from the boatshop to rip off an answer with his musket. After that the boat—a frigate—sailed back and forth, sounding with a lead, before splashing anchor. Captain 'Lon had been scraping the *Madrigal*'s bottom, meaning to paint before launching, and he brought a stool up so he could sit and watch the frigate. He surmised she was English, and he had an inkling as to what was afoot. In an hour or so a longboat moved around the stern of the frigate, into view, and came towards the estuary. Captain 'Lon said there was no doubt about it now—she was English. "Nobody ever could teach the English navy to row."

The longboat came by the wharf, but with exceeding formality not to it. The sailors backed water and held off, and the cox'n stood with cap in hand to speak his piece. "Commissioner Mavryck's compliments, and he requests permission to come ashore."

Captain 'Lon did the honors: "Name and hail, please,

and I'll thank you to inform the commissioner that he is welcome to Morning River and we await his pleasure."

"Thank you, sir—*Grimsby*, Portsmouth, King's orders, Boson Harvey at your service, sir."

Captain 'Lon seldom missed an opportunity like this one. His long unused lieutenancy would have been adequate, but now he promoted himself. "Captain Plaice here, Welcome all!" The boson saluted, the oarsmen picked up his measured stroke-stroke-stroke and the longboat moved down the estuary. The amenities had been impeccable, but the sweeps were catching some crabs. "What do you make of that?" asked Norman.

"I don't think an answer is hard," said 'Lon. "We're about to have a visitor, and I have some idea as to why. I know the man from long ago, and Elzada knows him. So does 'Chuck. And maybe you do—he's the man arranged to have you come here."

"Flanders?"

"Well, yes,"

"Ugliest man I ever saw—I better go warn Nora and the boys!"

The longboat came again, this time with two sea chests. Captain 'Lon led the way, and four seamen carried them up the path to the big house. "It's Mavryck," he said to Elzada, and Chuck said, "Oh, migawd!" On the third trip the longboat tied up and James Mavryck stepped ashore. Didn't he wear the uniform, though! It wasn't naval, and Captain 'Lon decided it was some king's livery outfit, meant for swagger and class, and perhaps to impress the natives. Extremely rich, and cunningly cut. Extravagant. By special appointment. The crimson tunic, embroidered, was partly subdued by the blue cape of short cut, and best of all was a fore-and-aft hat with a plume. Mavryck stood facing 'Lon and Norman, his back to the sailors, and he winked to belittle his own magnificence. Truth to tell, thought 'Lon, a rig like that does take the attention away from the face. Mavryck and 'Lon shook, and Mavryck and Norman shook, and Boson Harvey was dismissed to return the longboat to the *Grimsby*.

"There, by god! I can relax," said Mavryck. "Is there anybody in earshot so I have to be careful what I say?"

"Not a soul. Maybe you'll tell us why the hell you're here?"

"I will, I will. The game is going well and it's almost over, and now I believe the young lady of the Golden Clarion is under contract for a flip!" Mavryck looked like an Italian sunset coming towards the house, 'Lon and Norman with him, and Elzada let go her, "Jesus to Jesus!" Chuck stepped past her to set a pail on the doorstep.

"Beautiful! Beautiful!" Mavryck was saying, turning every few steps to look back over the ocean. "Norman, young man, I had no idea I was letting you into Paradise! You'll owe me a debt forever! A whole lifetime here! Beautiful!"

He picked up the pail from the steps, handed it to Chuck, and took the mug she had in her other hand.

"Thank you, thank you—and now, is it Miss Knight or Mrs. Plaice?"

Elzada gave him her hand. "Whichever it is, you're welcome to Morning River, and I'm glad to see you again!" He bowed.

"Now," he said. "Greetings over, I'm not comfortable in this jackanapes outfit, and I've no need here for the infernal dignity that goes with this uniform. Can't I shed, and feel human again?"

'Lon and Norman took the beckets on a chest and started to carry it up to Mavryck's room, but he said,

"No, not that one. That's the trousseau from the Boston Beddington. Plus, if you don't mind, a few other small things I've added on my own. Miss Beddington confided your measurements, Miss Elzada—and pleasant enough mathematics they are!—and unbeknownst to His Majesty they have been recorded in London and Paris. I took the liberty of spending some of His Majesty's supply to adorn your lovely back. Cheers!" He lifted his mug. 'Lon and Norman carried up the other chest, and Mavryck was gone for a time.

"What gives?" asked Elzada.

"There's a deal going on about who owns us—Dutch, French, English. This Mavryck—Norman knew him as Flanders, too—is land agent for the duke of York. He's been working for years to manipulate land titles and get everything lined up for the duke—that is, for the Crown. Chuck's father worked for him. So did Norman's. He didn't know it, but so did Achorn at the Golden Clarion. I've been running errands for him all over Hell's kitchen. All along the coast, he's had things lined up, and it's coming onto the time to pull the thing off—whatever it is. Here he comes."

Mavryck appeared, greatly subdued in appearance, and buttoning his leather jerkin. "There," he said. "Feel better!"

Saying he would like first to walk about and see the place, he added that one piece of news couldn't wait. "John Townes," he said.

"My uncle. Mother's younger brother. Lives in Salem, and I never did got to see him when I was in Boston."

"You never will. He died just before Christmas."

"I'm sorry!"

"You may not be too sorry. He was a wealthy man. He left no family. He left no will."

"What are you trying to tell us?"

"That Lawyer Blake knew he was your uncle, and he and Smart have entered your claim. In due time, whatever John Townes owned will be yours—except for what Blake and Smart steal. Even so, a good many Boston people are asking about this Elzada Knight . . . "

Captain 'Lon interrupted. "Under the circumstances, Elzada Plaice. We were married last winter by a rumdum priest Manny found somewhere."

Chuck said, "Nuptialed!"

"All right. I took the liberty of suggesting to Blake and Smart that they set up some kind of an agency to handle the Townes estate for now, and I've got papers to sign and get back to them. They need power of attorney. Unless you want to go to Boston and do your own business—which would ruin my summer plans to have you here. I suggest you sign."

Norman took Mavryck on a walk, starting up towards the cascade and then over the meadow. When they left, Chuck was looking at 'Lon and Elzada, and 'Lon said, "I married her money!" Chuck said, "Wel-l-l! If I'm to be lady's maid to your highness, I want a flunky to bring in wood and take out the slops!"

Elzada said—well, you know what Elzada said.

'Lon spoke again. "This Townes really was one of those things with a little French hat over it. In the same business I am, but I'm a minnow in his lake. Did almost all of his business through assistants, all over the place. He'd get something on a man and then blackmail him. Now and then one of his dupes would get caught, and Townes wouldn't lift a finger. Fact is, long ago, he damn' near caught me. The man didn't have a friend in the world—just money."

"And now it's all ours!" said Chuck.

"Well, we don't know that, yet—but seems to me, young lady, that you became a paid-up member of our benevolent society all of a sudden!" Elzada tickled her in the ribs and she giggled.

"Maybe I brought you luck!"

When Norman brought Mavryck back from the inspection tour, he was still more excited about the Morning River situation. "Except for stone construction, there's nothing like this in New York! Two houses like these? The mill, the boatworks, the barn, the wharf! Away off here? It's hard to believe. And look at that ocean!"

Supper was to be at the big house and the Kincaids would bring the two boys. As the flip appeared, there was accumulating evidence of a rabbit pie and, Chuck said, "with-its." Mavryck unfolded his story.

The duke of York wanted to make one continuous English colony from the Saint Croix to the Hudson. The duke had never been to America, and had no idea how preposterous this was. Mavryck, as his agent, had done his best to infiltrate Rhode Island and Massachusetts and get some support for the notion. Not a chance. Besides, there wasn't all that assurance that New York would be held—Parliament and Charles were botching things, and one little mistake . . . Mavryck said nothing treasonable, but put across the idea that the duke and Charles weren't inclined to listen to good advice.

The duke had also told Mavryck to get title to the eastern coast—beyond Massachusetts, and include that in his consolidated colony. That meant a dicker with France.

The rabbit pie was excellent. Long ago Jules Marcoux had shown Jabez, and then everybody else, how to set snares in the swamp, and Norman had taken over that department. There was never a lack of *lièvres* at Morning River Farm.

26

Chuck took the Kincaid boys and James Mavryck to the pool at the upper falls after breakfast, and a pail of brook trout ensued. Chuck took the boys to the wharf to instruct them in dressing fish, and Mavryck wandered over to help 'Lon scrape at the *Madrigal*. Nothing was said all morning about his reason to be at Morning River. The *Grimsby* stayed on anchor and there was no sign of activity aboard her. In the afternoon, Mavryck said he would like everybody to hear his instructions. Even to the boys.

"If things go as planned," he began, "some time in July we're going to have a big conference here, and I've been a long time getting ready for it. The duke of York wants the French to concede this part of The Maine to him, withdrawing all claims, so he can add it to his New York without stirring up anything." Mavryck shook his head as if to say the duke of York ought to know better.

Mavryck went on: "It was back when you went to Boston, Elzada, that things clicked. 'Lon told me about Morning River, and I knew it was the right place. 'Lon sent you to Achorn's so I could find you. Achorn didn't know it at the time, but because I thought I could use him I had him set up with the Golden Clarion. Your father knew Achorn, Chuck, and so did yours, Norman. Now, Rufus Achorn will come to Morning River about the first of July, and he will be the official interpreter for this conference. It is critical that none of you knows him or ever heard of him. He will come as a stranger and know none of you. And, Elzada, you will, until the conference is over, forget absolutely that you know any French."

"Rufus Achorn knows I do."

"He'll forget that. The French delegates who come must believe that Rufus is the only one on our side that understands their language. This is important, and don't make any slips!"

"Je comprends!"

"Fine. Now, it has been carefully arranged that none of the French delegates knows English and none of the English knows any French. The whole scheme will blow up otherwise. Clear?"

"Not very. You make it sound as if I'm to be in on the conference."

"You are. You all are. I want the six delegates to think they are welcome guests in your home—keep away from formality, politics, protocol. Just a happy family that has opened its doors, and right here on The Maine that we're talking about. So, let the boys run in and out, and go about as usual, and every afternoon we'll have a flip session with Chuck and a banquet with you, Elzada, as gracious hostess. Alternating, I insist, the London and Paris styles donated by His Most Gracious Britannic Majesty. I think the Englishmen who come may keep dignified, but if the Frenchmen are the palace leeches I think they are you don't want to get caught in a corner.

So this is my plan, and it's got to work! It's the most important thing in my life. The Frenchmen will come from Chignecto during the first week of July, and the English from New York about the same. The delegates will stay on the ships, but will come to this house each afternoon for talks, sociability, and supper. And Chuck!"

Chuck started as if slapped, and looked everywhere except at Monster Mavryck.

"In the chest with Elzada's things are some fancies for you. I didn't bring anything for Nora because I didn't have her size—but I see now she can get into one of yours. You, Chuck, are going to become famous back in France as the flip expert, and you're close enough to a grown woman to begin with the wily arts. Be charming, and push the flip. Do you know how to serve a wine?"

Chuck looked helplessly at Elzada, and then turned to stare point blank at Mavryck. Elzada said, "She will know if she doesn't. I've got a book on French wines."

Mavryck again: "The wine, and everything else we're going to need for our banquets will come either with Achorn, or I'll bring them when I come. You've got the Salerno china; crystal is on the way. Corkscrew?"

"No home on The Maine is without one."

Chuck said, "I still don't believe one word I'm hearing!"

"You better. If this thing comes off I'll be indebted to all of you more than you'll believe, ever."

James Mavryck stood up, went behind his chair, and put his hands to its back. "The skulduggery I've just outlined is the biggest cutthroat shenanigan ever thought up in the history of diplomacy—we're all actors in a play, and we've got to make Morning River believed."

He smiled—the smile that seemed to dislocate his skull.

27

Mavryck stayed at Morning Farm three days, wandering about to admire the springtime, helping with readying the *Madrigal,* and playing with the trout. He said the crew of the *Grimsby* would expect him to stay a week, and so would be pleased at an earlier departure. He brought a pistol from his sea chest, and soon after he fired it the longboat of the *Grimsby* appeared. This morning Mavryck had on his sunset-and-rainbow uniform, his plume meticulously positioned. Boson Harvey helped him to a thwart, and with a "See you soon!" Commissioner Mavryck was down the estuary and away. When he was beyond earshot, Elzada said, "You know, his looks sort of grow on you."

Chuck said, "They sure as hell grew on him!"

"Oh, Chuck! You know—after a while you forget his looks. The man has everything except beauty. But as you say, 'Lon, I'd hate to have him for an enemy."

"Right now you have him for a friend, and he's got us in the palm of his hand. I'd worry about what he's got us into, except that I trust him from away back."

Manny the Portygee was due day to day, and when

he arrived he brought the two islanders and the *Madrigal* was easily afloat. Captain 'Lon picked up his crew boys after their winter on Monhegan Island, provisioned at Pemaquid, and was off to The Islands with smokers, corned hake, and salt fishpeas. Good paying cargo. Norman worked in the boatshop, but as May warmed into June he worked with the gardens. He exercised his young steers a little every day, and by fall they should be ready for heavy work. He needed logs for the mill. The *Madrigal* was gone just short of a month and came up the estuary on an afternoon tide. Captain 'Lon was featherwhite about something, and hardly waited for the *Madrigal* to touch the wharf. He was on the run up the path to the big house. The crew boys took the *Madrigal* down to deep water for the customary rendezvous with Manny the Portygee.

Elzada and Chuck met Captain 'Lon at the door, and while his greeting was hearty, it was brief. He looped an arm about the waist of each, hustled them holterbolter onto two chairs, and wagging a finger at Elzada he shouted, "John Townes! That Double-B-Boston-Bahstid! What did you know about him, anyway?"

"Not a thing. I never saw him in my life! My mother never saw him this side of England."

"Well, your mother sure did two things right in this world! One was having you, and the other was picking the right brother! Your John Townes died worth three million pounds!"

"Jes . . . " Elzada, being seated, could only stand. She stood up. Captain 'Lon sat down. Chuck didn't move.

The boys had run up to the meadow to tell Norman that Captain 'Lon was home, and he came into the kitchen to find the three of them looking at nothing with blank eyes. Elzada found her voice first.

"And now for the good news! Do we get any of it?"

"You do. Don't you remember? I nuptialed off in favor of old Money-Bags Kincaid, here? You better tell him the news—I can't bear to look at him! No, I don't mean that—Hi, Norman! I bring tidings that you are a millionare, thank me!"

Captain 'Lon had a sheaf of papers for Elzada to sign, and he was to make a special trip with them back to Boston. He said, "We need your father's will, birth records, anything we can find. You're big shebang of a trust set up called the Townes Estate. Your two solicitors, associates, assistants, hangers-on, schemers—Smart and Blake—they don't need to steal from you. They can live on what money gets spilled on the floor. They even hire lawyers now to do their legal work! You've got two of the shrewdest bandits in Boston making you money so fast you can't count it! And who do you think has his eye on them—Jim Mavryck! He gave them blank-cart to go ahead, and first thing they did was borrow on profits in escrow and buy three new ships."

"Blank-cart! Why are they buying ships?"

"Expanding."

"That's not what I mean—why can't Norman build ships?"

"Jesus to Jesus, Elzada! You don't pay attention. Norman's got your name on a little piece of paper, and he don't have to lift a finger! It's poor Chuck and me, downright paupers in this company."

And it was even so. Captain 'Lon was careful to be sure that Norman knew he was joshing, and Chuck helped with this by offering to lend a few pennies to anybody in want. Captain 'Lon sailed early the next morning with the signed papers and records from Jabez's old strongbox. He had time enough to return to Morning River before the conference.

28

When Captain 'Lon had delivered the papers to Smart and Blake, and they assured him they had what they needed, he bought what windows he could find in Boston and loaded them into the *Madrigal*. Windows were in good demand all down the coast, where settlers could make about everything they needed except glass. Glass must be transported edges up—never laid flat—and the crew boys were carefully stowing cargo. Rufus Achorn appeared, and if anybody had perceived his approach, or been near enough to hear his words, he would be certain that Rufus Achorn and Captain Plaice had never heard of each other before.

"I understand you are sailing to The Maine?"

"That's right!"

"I have business there. Would you have an accommodation?"

"I think we can make room. Whereabouts you bound?"

There was no attempt to be cozy. Mavryck had said Rufus would appear as a stranger, so 'Lon played the game. Rufus had spoken loud and clear, so if overheard he would appear to be that stranger. 'Lon knew perfectly well what Rufus was about to say. He said, "Far down."

The *Madrigal* put off the windows at Falmouth, and came to Morning River with Rufus aboard. His meeting with Elzada and Chuck was also dissembled. Elzada thought, "Chicanery!" and she and Chuck dutifully made believe they had never set eyes on the man. Chuck took him to the corner room opposite hers, and Captain 'Lon helped him set his sea chest at the foot of the bed. For nearly a week Rufus came to his meals, stayed in his room, took a daily constitutional up into the meadow, and made no conversation. Mavryck had said they were all play actors.

The Frenchmen arrived.

The vessel, gun ports closed in a gesture of peace, hove into view and executed a magnificent maneuver of taking down sail and anchoring. Captain 'Lon was fascinated. "Just like somebody playing a flute!" There had been no signal, such as the *Grimsby* had made when Mavryck came, so Norman came from the boatshop and touched off his musket. Allowing time for the sound to cross the water, there followed great stir on the warship's fantail, and from Morning River Farm the sailors could be seen making ready their response. When the small cannon blew its puff of smoke astern, the sailors ran to the rail to look up at Morning Farm. *La Diadème* had brought the king's agents to confer with the English.

Jim Mavryck had things in hand. Later in the afternoon H.M.S. *Honour* arrived, blowing her signal gun just as she turned Outer Razor Ledge to come into the reach. Again, the French were caught unready, and a second scurry came at the taffrail before the gun spoke. In less than an hour the *Grimsby* appeared, blowing her signal and getting response from *Honour* and *Diadème* and Norman Kincaid, and right away Mavryck was brought to the Morning River wharf in the longboat.

"All set," he said. "Now, we'll make with the polites out there for now, and we'll come ashore tomorrow afternoon for the parley. I'm here now just to check on Achorn. He's here?"

"In his fairyland of make-believe!"

"Fine!" Mavryck stepped into the longboat and was returned to the *Grimsby*. That afternoon the *Grimsby*'s longboat moved back and forth between the *Honour* and the *Diadème*, and the Morning River spectators assumed that hands were shaken, bows accomplished, and courtesies exchanged. "My guess," said Captain 'Lon, "is that the English have made a presentation of rich and impressive English goods for the Frenchies to take back to their king and queen, and the Frenchies have kindly reciprocated with three cases of wine meant to be drunk here."

The next morning the longboat of the *Grimsby* made three trips to bring supplies to the wharf—including three cases of wine with French labels. The sailors trudged back and forth to the big house, and Elzada and Chuck supervised storage. On the fourth trip Jim Mavryck came, now in another splendid regalia—he was to eat at the big house at noon, confer with Rufus Achorn, and then post himself at the wharf as conference chairman and receptionist to the delegates. Captain 'Lon was to stand with him. Rufus was to be held back until later. "Let 'em fumble—we'll find out how we stand. If we get an Englishman who knows French or a Frenchman who knows English, we've done a year's work for nothing."

"Whoopsie-DOO!" shouted Chuck when Elzada appeared in her Paris gown, and then she and Nora went to change. The three French agents came first. None responded in any way to the English 'Lon and Jim used to greet them. They stood back, uneasy, and Norman motioned to escort them up the path to the big house.

All of a size, all shaven except for identical mustaches, all in the same lavish uniform of the Royal Household, they stood three abreast inside the kitchen as Elzada welcomed them—in English. "Welcome, welcome!"

"Merci, madame," three voices with one remark. They bowed, and each in turn bussed Elzada's hand, each making the little "Oomph!" sound as punctuation. Chuck had mugs ready, and one of the agents—the one on Chuck's right—said something in French which made Chuck turn to Elzada as if for assistance. Elzada shrugged her shoulders. The man had asked what the drink might be, but he would get no answer until Rufus appeared. Each agent had bowed with his name. They had done this on the wharf with 'Lon and Norman, but neither had understood. Elzada feigned otherwise, but she learned their names:

"Alphe Moreau du Gas." He bowed again.

"Denis d'Essagne." He bowed again.

"Robert-Louis Delorme." He bowed again.

Elzada shrugged again at Chuck, spread her hands as baffled, and said again, "Welcome, welcome."

When the English came, Mavryck allowed time enough to assure himself none of them knew French, and came leading them to the house. Rufus appeared, and after that things were comfortable. He introduced everybody, and Elzada marveled at the ease with which he shifted from tongue to tongue.

"Fitzwilliams," he said.

"Enchanté!"

"Delorme," he said.

"How-ja-do!"

The second Englishman was a Scot named Mac-
Eachern, and the third was introduced as James Stuart.
He seemed faintly Scottish, too. The conference had
begun. Chuck and Nora attended the mugs, and soon
Rufus answered the question about flip. "Gentlemen,"
said Mavryck at last, and Rufus translated along with
him, "we are here on an important mission, and while
we must never shirk our social duties, we should organ-
ize and agree on procedure."

Nothing was accomplished that first afternoon. Each
delegate had a little speech to make—his message from
his king, his delight at being present, the honor involved,
gratitude to the Plaice family, admiration of the scen-
ery. When Fitzwilliams inserted an extemporaneous
appreciation of flip, Rufus translated and the three
Frenchmen replied, "Vive le fleep!"

The afternoon was gone by the time Rufus finished
translating these remarks, and while Elzada and the two
girls made the table ready, 'Lon and Norman showed
the delegates about the place, Rufus attending. Elzada
heard Delorme exclaim, from the back room, "Here, in
America—a library like this? Incredible!" Fitzwilliams
asked what was said, and Rufus translated. Then Fitzwilliams said, "Yes, tell me, Mavryck—how do these
people come by such books, so far away?"

Captain 'Lon took over and explained about small
coasting vessels along The Maine, and how just about
anything could be had by waiting long enough. Then,
when Rufus put that in French, there was almost a bust-
up of the language bit. Delorme asked, "Yes, but the
French titles—who reads the books in French?" Elzada
had come by now, and Rufus seemed somewhat relieved.

He translated for her. She smiled. "Oh, yes. Years ago we had a French family down at the other house. In my father's time." Rufus put that into French. That Elzada had been reading from the French book about French wines that very morning, to tell Chuck how to serve, was not divulged.

You'd have sworn Chuck learned to serve wine in her infancy. Chilled in the bubbling spring up the hill, two bottles, for starters, were brought down by Norman. Holding the first in a napkin, Chuck presented it to Alphé Moreau du Gas, who studied the label with keen interest, as if he'd never seen one before, and at last nodded approval. She gave Fitzwilliams the chance to do the same, which he did. Looking at Elzada for a nod of approval, Chuck then drew the cork, and sniffed it, holding her head a bit askew as if in deep contemplation of an abstruse subject. She poured a taste in one of the sparkling glasses Mavryck had just brought in the *Grimsby*, and set it before Delorme. He seemed to pass into a trance after a sip, but was able to rally, and finally spoke. Rufus translated.

"You may serve it."

After supper, Rufus appeared with pipes, and nobody asked how come so many pipes when 'Lon and Norman didn't smoke. With every evidence of *bonhomie* and hearty good fellowship, the group broke up just before sunset and the delegates returned to their vessels for the night. Jim Mavryck was last to go. He paused at the kitchen door to put his hands on Elzada's shoulders and to say, "Well done!" He stepped down the path toward the wharf, where the longboat was waiting.

Tomorrow would be the day.

29

Afterwards Elzada could never say just when it was she "smelled a rat." Playing her part as official hostess, she was in and out of the room where the men were talking, and she heard a word here and a word there without paying too much attention to what was being said. Now and then she'd stay in the kitchen with Chuck and Nora and lose all continuity. Mavryck had said the purpose of the conference was to get England undisputed title to her—Elzada's—part of The Maine, to bring that part of *l'Acadie* away from France. To add it to the holdings of the duke of York. But now, as she was coming and going, she heard something about the money France was to pay England. This stopped her short. Shouldn't it be the other way around? Must have heard wrong.

She looked into the conference room and the delegates were intent. Fitzwilliams, Stuart, MacEachern were leaning forward to hear the translation Rufus was about to make; du Gas, d'Essagne, and Delorme were settled back confidently seeming to have an advantage. Mavryck, as chairman but not a delegate, sat to one side, seemingly paying little attention, if not half asleep. Elzada now realized that what she had heard about a payment had been spoken in French

   . . . forget absolutely that you know any French.

She heard in her memory Mavryck's voice as he spoke on his first visit to Morning River.

She withdrew to the kitchen, but returned at once to tidy the sideboard, and now she paid good attention. Rufus was translating, and Elzada considered his English a trifle, at least, at odds with the French she had just heard. On the next exchange, she knew! Rufus was deliberately, and with great skill, mistranslating! For that matter, he wasn't translating at all—he was giving each side just about the opposite of what the other side had said, and he was doing it calmly, with complete poise, with scholarly attitude.

The man is a crook!

Stuart was saying, "True, the payment for Dunkirk was liberal, and His Majesty is grateful. But here we have another matter—Dunkirk was close and distance can distort. We beg you to look into the future—imagine the wealth, the forests, the fisheries, the minerals . . ." Stuart spread his hands and paused. Perfectly clear—Mavryck had lied! Instead of coming to bargain for *l'Acadie*, the goddamn duke of York was trying to sell it! Haggling at a price. Rufus translated, and Elzada was truly baffled. He gave the French no approximation of what Stuart had said!

   . . . forget absolutely that you know any French.

Elzada went to the kitchen.

The supper, after the conference, was in the same

fine degree as the afternoon before, but the company was cool and subdued. The Frenchmen paid court to Elzada, Nora, and Chuck as before, but were indifferently polite to the English delegates and Mavryck. Mavryck, appearing to pick up the mood of the English delegates, was downcast. He was offering comfort to them, but it seemed to do no good. The discovery of Rufus's treachery subdued Elzada too, but she made a hostess's effort to keep jolly. Why the hell couldn't she catch the eye of that wopple-jawed Mavryck and signal him into the shed? Why had Rufus disappeared? Jesus to Jesus!

Elzada sent Chuck up to call Rufus to supper, but he wasn't in his room.

Before the meal was over, things were sticky indeed. Without Rufus, there was no French-English, and diplomatic good taste forbade each side to socialize with itself. Mavryck, grumpy and morose, even surly, only grunted when he got up and left early. The Frenchmen lingered, not only to let the Englishmen go first, but to permit some polite murmurings to the ladies. Dumb as a doorknob, Elzada shrugged and shrugged at them.

Elzada broke the rules and told 'Lon in bed. She held him close, whispering, and he said, "Beats me!" It beat him so much that he stared into the darkness for some time, occasionally saying, "Beats me!" Elzada was restless even when she dozed off.

La Diadème sailed at sunrise, disdaining the courtesy of a salute. After a discreet interval, the *Honour* followed. She, too, failed to signal. "And all that for nothing!" said 'Lon. "A jeezly damn' bust!" The *Grimsby* stayed at anchor, and come breakfast time her longboat appeared and Mavryck was put ashore. 'Lon went down to meet him, and at the same time Rufus came from the

boatshop, where he had spent the night. It shook 'Lon
when Mavryck and Rufus embraced like long-lost friends
on the wharf, clapped each other on the back, and
laughed at their own private joke—whatever it was.
Mavryck, this morning, was without his shine and sheen,
and wore good colonial garb with a leather cap—which
he doffed at 'Lon, and grinned a happy good morning
with all the charm of a pine stump. 'Lon was shaking
his head as the three walked up to the house, and Elzada
had the creeps as she faced the duty of squealing to
Mavryck about Achorn. And then—then it came to her
with a pop! She knew they knew! They knew she knew.
She, not Mavryck, had been the dupe. The men came
into the kitchen, and Elzada said to Mavryck, "I'd hate
to have you for an enemy!"

Mavryck bowed as low as a man might without losing
his balance, so his leather cap against his chest almost
brushed the floor. He straightened up, took Elzada's
hand, and spoke to her confidentially, "Mon amour! Je
sais parler français depuis plus de quarante-cinq ans!"
Rufus was holding in, but only just.

'Lon said, "What the hell?"

Elzada said, "Well Jesus to Jesus!"

"Elzada, you were wonderful. I had a bad moment
when you discovered what Rufus was doing, but it was
nothing to the bad moment he had! The thing got out
of hand there for a spell, and he was improvising. Now,
children, do you have any questions?"

"Of course we have questions. Shall we eat?"

"First," Mavryck said, "this Stuart really is the duke
of York. I tried to keep him out of the picture, but he's
the king's brother and I don't go around giving orders
to a king's brother. When the king gave him New York,
he sent me and some flunkies over here to run his show.

He's not really a good boy, and wants to make everybody a pope. He told me to annex Massachusetts; can
you imagine a Catholic Massachusetts? And the Dutch—
well, it was a job and what I did I did well. The idea to
get title to The Maine from the French was on the level—
he meant that, and I was working on it. Then a comical
thing happened."

"How were your eggs?" asked Chuck.

"The first two were fine."

"Right up!"

"King Charles," Mavryck went on, "is said to be
extremely witty, which is a half truth. When he can't
get any play money out of Parliament, he wheedles some
from Louis of France, and all at once he got the notion
to sell The Maine to Louis—price to be discussed. I've
got the thing pretty well sewed up for the duke just the
other way around when I'm told to come about."

"You stop waving that fork around like a pickerel spear,
and I'll renew your assets," said Chuck.

"Thank you, Chuck. You will be remembered forever as the girl who put flip into the French language!"

"Now, let's see . . . Yes, meantime I find myself in
love with America. The king is a chump, and his brother
is a fool. I decide, somewhere along the line, that this
land we're talking about shouldn't belong to a king—
but to the people who are going to live on it and call it
home. And now I've had a talk with 'Lon, here, and the
story of Morning River Farm pleases me. I can't be treasonable against Charles and James, but I can conve-
niently turn out to be a lousy diplomat. By the time I
decide what it is I have to do, I'm all set up and ready
to do it. Morning Farm, Elzada, Norman, Rufus—even
the flip girl. All I have to do is go ahead and hold the
conference, and have it blow up."

Rufus spoke. "I never knew until a short time ago that the commissioner made it possible for me to move to Boston. I was most unhappy at New York after the English."

Mavryck again: "It was great fun! Elzada, do you know that the *Grimsby* made a special trip to get your hostess dresses? No, you wouldn't. Well, we made some history, and I've cast my lot with the colonies. My resignation as the duke's nose wiper is following him home on the *Grimsby*. I guess that clears everything up."

"Not all the way," said Elzada. "What happens if they smell you in the woodwork?"

"Doubtful. The old proverb runs that people who steal wood together are friends for life. Rufus and I stole some wood; Morning River and I stole some wood. I'm not worrying. King Charles may wonder, but he and the duke have their hands full without bird-dogging me. I think I'm going to grow old here in New England, healthy and happy, the homeliest man in the world. I plan to come every May and eat a pan of trout with you—maybe oftener—welcome guest in the charming home of the richest woman on The Maine."

"You'll always be welcome. But the richest woman on The Maine has a surprise for the homeliest man in the world—I hold this land here under deed from the French crown."

"How can that be?"

"It's a long story for another time. It shows that French-English conferences are nothing new to Morning Farm."

"Maybe so, but this one we just had is the important one. I doubt if history will give you credit for saving The Maine for England—but that's what you did. You foiled a foolish king who wanted to give it away. But you've got an English deed, too—Blake told me that. Talk about playing the middle against both ends!"

"Where will you be?" asked Elzada.

"Here and there. Captain 'Lon can find me. And Rufus can always set out a bucket."

30

The let-down after the conference was expressed by Chuck: "I go around feeling what happened, anyway?" Mavryck sailed on the *Grimsby* two mornings after the delegates left, and the wind breezed up immediately from the west. Captain 'Lon went around with a smile, thinking about the poor sailors working that frigate by the wind. They might make Monhegan in two days. It turned out to be one of those down-Maine "three-day-blows," so he revised that to four days the next morning. Mavryck wouldn't let Achorn travel with him on the *Grimsby*—said the captain was a stickler for the log and even set down when he used the bucket. He didn't want anything in the record that showed he and Rufus were that close. So Rufus stayed, pleasuring himself. He spent a good bit of time with Norman, particularly in the boatshop, and he enjoyed going down along the flats for clams. Mavryck had found somebody to run the Golden Clarion, so Rufus was in no hurry. He went up to Boston in August.

Captain 'Lon and the *Madrigal* kept a fairly constant

schedule of three weeks to The Islands and back. Even
with contrary weather he could hold close to that. Elzada
was pleased and Chuck was I-told-you-so that his stop-
overs at Morning River became longer and longer. Two
days became three, three five, and in late summer he
stayed three weeks to help Norman with the harvest.
Chuck almost died a-laughin' when she looked out one
morning and saw the Old Salt teaming Norman's steers.
As Chuck joshed Elzada about Captain 'Lon's hanging
around, and "I can't imagine why!" Elzada took notice
that Chuck was something of a beautiful young lady.
But Elzada was not the first to notice; Ginger Pitcher,
of the *Madrigal* crew, began to spark her, and the longer
Captain 'Lon stayed each time at Morning River, the
more Chuck saw of Ginger Pitcher. Chuck told Elzada
about it and said, "What do you think?"

"I think good. Don't do anything foolish, because you
don't need to. Let's ask Captain 'Lon for a run down on
the boy, and we'll talk it over. He still has bound time,
so I doubt he's anything laid by—and bear in mind,
Chuck, that you're not a poor woman. Always be the
lady—it makes you feel good with yourself, and it's good
for everybody."

As to the affairs of Morning River Farm, Elzada had
said to 'Lon, "I haven't spoken to Nora yet, but I will—
this is what I'd like: I'd like for you and Chuck, one day
a week, to go down to the other house and have supper
with Nora and the boys. Norman's to come up and he'll
have supper with me. We'll have our business meeting,
and after supper everybody comes to the big house for
the evening." It turned out to be Wednesday.

Schooling was put on schedule, too. Every day, rain
or shine, the boys came for their lessons, and as Chuck
and Nora joined in this, Elzada sent for more books.

They came, in a crate from John Townes Estate, and Norman brought it ashore with his hoist on the wharf.

One Wednesday at supper, Elzada suggested perhaps Norman would care to spend some time in Boston, learning something of the Townes business, but he wouldn't listen. Not for him. And then word came in late fall that James Mavryck had joined Smart and Blake to become general manager of Townes Estate. On his last voyage before hauling the *Madrigal* for the winter, Captain 'Lon paused in Boston to look into this, and he reported that Mavryck was happy as a high-water clam, glad to be shut of the politics of his commissionership, and with him in the saddle Smart and Blake had nothing to do but sit around and count money. 'Lon told Norman that Smart and Blake wanted him to build each of them a sloop—a play boat to ride around in, maybe thirty feet or so. Norman said, "Let's see—I do the work, and I use Morning Farm lumber. They buy two sloops, using Morning Farm money. What kind of a deal is this?" But he did make the two sloops that winter. He said he had thought the matter over very carefully, and decided Elzada could afford them. The two sloops were made from a new pattern that Norman worked on for weeks. Later, he fastened his half model to a board and nailed it to the boatshop wall. That was to become the Kincaid Sloop, standard for a generation along the down-east coast. Norman made dozens of them, and later his boys made dozens more.

After Elzada had told 'Lon about Ginger Pitcher's yen for Chuck, all he said was, "Son of a gun!"

But soon, as if on sudden impulse, he found a chance and said to Chuck, "I'll have words with you." You know very well that Chuck knew why, but she feigned and said, "What about?"

"How's about this Ginger Pitcher?"

"He likes my haddock chowder. Wants to change my name."

"Well, I suppose anything would be better than Chuck. Have you stopped to think about children?"

"Not hardly."

"Well, you and Ginger are going to have some funny looking ones."

"Oh?"

"Don't you remember—little Pitchers have big ears? Now, I haven't had a chance to speak to Ginger, but see what you think. You understand, Elzada and I have no special responsibility for you, but we realize you're the closest to a daughter we'll have. But, Elzada had her arrangement with Norman, and you know all about that. She doesn't plan to let you down, and I won't. What I'm trying to say is that you've got a lot more going for you right now than Ginger has. He's a good boy, my favorite. He's ready right now for his own vessel, but he's still apprenticed. Point I'm making—he hasn't a farthing. Understand?"

"Yes."

"Well, you think I'm going to ask you to forget him. I'm not. Good boys looking for pretty wives don't make crowds anywhere, let alone here. The *Madrigal* is an old boat, but good for a while yet—maybe we can use her in a deal."

"A deal?"

"A deal. Suppose next spring I was to turn the *Madrigal* over to Ginger on some kind of percentage, and let him try his hand with her to The Islands? Let him sail her and let him handle the business. See how he does. Manny will give him a start. I'll have to sign him off on his apprenticeship, and he'll have to take on some responsibilities. If he can bring the *Madrigal* home every month or so with a profit—you willing to wait and see?"

"Oh, sure!"

"There's more. We got to think of a place for you to live. Monhegan Island's no place. So sooner or later you have a talk with Elzada and Norman, and see what they think about a third house here. Some day, I think Elzada and I will be glad to have you around. No hurry. And another thing—enough for now—If Ginger does well with the *Madrigal*, when she hogs out Elzada can fix him up with our friend Mavryck."

Chuck said, "When I bawl I like to be alone," and she went around the big house towards the upper falls.

31

"She'll fetch more in The Islands than she will up here," Captain 'Lon said at breakfast. "How about a jaunt down to Antigua and we'll buccaneer back home?"

"Now what?"

"The *Madrigal*. She's going to need a lot of work if we keep her. Ginger hasn't abused her a bit, but she's full of years. It's going to be like tearing out my heart, but what else should we do—beach her out and watch her rot? Somebody down in The Islands can get a few years from her yet."

"When does Ginger take over the *Pertinax*?"

"She's due to launch in September, but he'll tie up the *Madrigal* in August. You and I can take the *Madrigal* for one last ride, drop Ginger off at North Yarmouth to wait on the *Pertinax*, and keep on going. Sell the *Madrigal*, come home on one of your rum barges, and settle in for dotage and senility."

"Somehow," said Elzada, "I can't picture you and us without the *Madrigal*."

"She's been a good boat and made a lot of money. But everything has a season. I ache to part with her, but I've sort of made arrangements. I'm pretty sure I know a buyer. Then, after you and I get enough of The Islands, we'll come home and Norman is to show me the tricks and I'm going to make a sloop for myself. Something for around here, but stanch enough to make a trip to Boston. Something I can sail alone, and take you cod lining. Any objections?"

Manny the Portygee never figured, as Captain 'Lon had suggested, in giving Ginger a leg up with the *Madrigal*. The old smuggler disappeared. No reason to suspect other than "lost at sea"—the big mistake. Captain 'Lon took the sailing dory and went over off and on to visit with the two islanders who had lived with Manny in their little three-cabin village. They joked about all of Manny's henchmen who were high and dry now that Manny didn't come to buy, sell, swap—and pay them off. Captain 'Lon gave a thought to Father Hermadore. But a year passed, and the islanders were bereft without Manny. Norman found work for them to do and they came by the day to help him in the shop or in the gardens. They knew how to slaughter, too, and Norman had never cared for that. One of them took over the boatshop forge, and when he said he knew how to shoe a horse, Norman sent for a horse.

Ginger's acceptance of Captain 'Lon's proposal had been prompt. Cap in hand, Ginger had asked Captain 'Lon for Chuck, and Captain 'Lon had asked him what Chuck thought about that.

"I don't rightly know, sir, but I thought I'd shovel the path before I walked in. We've spoke, and that's about all. It's not just your permission I'd want, sir, but your advice, too."

You can't beat that kind of soft-soaping, and the arrangements were made. Ginger did well with the *Madrigal*, and now the Townes Estate was building him a tops'l schooner, the *Pertinax*. Chuck went around in her dream, and whistled so much Elzada finally spoke to her about it. Well, she said, "Gawd's sake, Chuck, can't you hum some?"

So now the *Madrigal* was on her way to The Islands again, with Captain 'Lon again at the tiller. Ginger was dropped off, and two days later 'Lon asked Elzada if she wanted to pause in Boston and look into her interests. Beside him at the tiller she stretched on her toes, kissed his ear, and said, "I also have interests in the Loo'ards."

They went well around Cape Cod.

They had, as Elzada told Chuck after getting back to Morning River, "one helluva good time!" Everybody knew Captain 'Lon. By now, Ginger was known, too, and many asked for him. At Cayes, Captain 'Lon pointed at two ships tied to the sugar dock, and he told Elzada, "There's two very special vessels!"

"Why special?"

"They're yours."

And the buyer did buy. The *Madrigal* changed hands as soon as 'Lon and Elzada were sure of passage home on a Townes Estate vessel. Norfolk, New York, Boston, Falmouth, and after two days in Falmouth Captain 'Lon found places on a Banker. The fishermen out of Boston knew nothing about the haddock hole at Halfway Rock, and when Captain 'Lon put them over it, Elzada made a haddock chowder—haddock chowder being known in the family for some time now as a Chuck Chowder. The fishermen didn't know about Morning River, and were pleased to learn of anchorage behind the Razor Islands. Yes, they had known Manny the Portygee.

While Captain 'Lon and Elzada were getting ashore, Norman talked to the fishing skipper, and got his order for a nest of ten dories.

32

The second year after the sale of the *Madrigal*, Captain 'Lon was still working on his sloop. Norman had finished four in the same time. And the dories. Captain 'Lon called his labor "playing around with my boat," and often confirmed his own retirement by saying, "I'm not going anywhere—gives me something to do." He was no hand at tools, and Norman patiently encouraged him and wouldn't let him leave a thing until it was right. 'Lon heard Norman say, "Hello! What's this?" and looked up to see a ketch easing to the wharf. Off the ketch stepped James Mavryck—as if there could be any mistake about *him*. He had come at last for his promised Maytime renunion with the Morning River trout, an appointment he was to keep faithfully for many years to come. Norman looked the ketch over critically—she was a lovely boat, well crafted. "Handsome little vessel," he said when he joined 'Lon and Mavryck after the two crewmen had shown him below.

"Like her?"

"Oh, yes."

"Might be the owner'd give her to you."

"Well, I don't know as I'd care to own her, but I like her lines. Who's the owner?"

"Woman named Elzada Plaice—that's the harbor boat from the Townes Estate. Use her to chandler ships at Boston."

Mavryck did have his go at the trout, but his visit to Morning River Farm was also on business. He began with Chuck. What would Chuck think about living in Boston? If he took Ginger Pitcher on as his understudy in the management of Townes Estate, he'd be based in Boston, and would she want to leave The Maine? Said he hadn't talked to Ginger about this yet, thinking Chuck should mull it over first. Chuck said, "Holy old trumpets!"

But his big business was with Elzada. At Wednesday supper, he sat with Norman and Elzada and they listened to a fairly long recitation. "That meeting we had here over who owns The Maine gets more important all the time. We saved the country from France and for the English, but it turns out we saved it mostly for ourselves.

"Well, it takes so long to get back and forth across the ocean. When our little conference broke up, everybody got home to find there was precious little interest in matters over here. Charles, playing the big European game, kept on trying to shove the pope down throats, then Parliament put in a bill to keep Catholics off the throne, and our boy the duke knew that meant him. He got Charles to send Parliament home, but about that time word leaked out that Charles and James had been in cahoots to give The Maine away. Wonder how that got around? Some people weren't happy about that, and they're trying to bring about a good and permanent settlement between Massachusetts and The Maine. I think it'll come about. When it does, you, Townes Estate— myself—will be sitting pretty."

"You've cast your lot with us?"

"No other way. King's bidding is no kind of a job, and governments are poor benefactors. I'm letting you be my benefactress, dear lady, and now to the meat: We need to stop lugging all our eggs around in one basket."

"So?"

"Spread out. Right in The Maine we can make a lot of sound investments."

"Like?"

"We're surrounded by opportunity. Land. We've got a couple of dozen settlements in The Maine now, and they've got to grow. Now and then an Indian whoops, but the militia is doing a better job, and things have quieted down. Buy land for miles around every settlement. Then wait."

"How do you go about getting this land?"

"Like hiving a swarm of bees—very cautiously. Have everything in the poke before anybody knows what you're up to. Set up a dummy company, borrow on Townes Estate assets. I can find an agent to run the dummy."

"What else?"

"Water rights. Find all the places for dams up and down all these rivers. Every settlement needs a grinding mill. And a sawmill. Sew up as many dam privileges as you can find. Another dummy."

"And?"

"Fisheries. Fisheries has always been big, but nobody big has been in fisheries. Build bigger boats, salt more fish, expand—and hire Townes Estate to deliver in your own bottoms. And bottoms—get into shipbuilding. There's no limit to that. We've got lumber, power to saw it, men like Norman to build, and men like 'Lon to sail. Finance construction with Townes Estate money. Follow me?"

"Over a devious route—what do you say? Norman? And we'll want to hear what 'Lon thinks."

"With nods from them," Mavryck said, "I'll get our legal department to draw up dummy papers, and . . ."

"Legal department? What became of Smart and Blake?"

"Them! Now *they* hire lawyers. Then they go sailing. Thanks to me, they can go—but don't discount those two! They're as loyal to you as they're beholden to me! They like prosperity."

The folks came up from the lower house, then, and the rest of the evening was family. Mavryck asked 'Lon if he knew much about bananas—reason was, he thought 'Lon would make the right dummy to run the Guatemalan banana company the Townes Estate was about to form. 'Lon said he'd like that job. "Right now," he said, "I'm rubbing beach sand and pogy oil on a cheeserind, and the way Norman holds my nose to the work I'm tied up for another five years—but after that it would be good to get away."

Chuck said she heard somewhere that down in the banana country they use ripe bananas to grease the ways when they launch a boat. "We can sell ourselves our own bananas!"

"My gollies, girl," said Mavryck, "you got a head on your shoulders! Thinking every minute!"

Chuck said, "What became of your monkey suit?"

"Don't you monkey suit me! Wait till you see that Ginger of yours in the captain's uniform of Townes

Estate. We got a house livery that makes the First Lord of the Admiralty look like a haystack. He's just too good to be true. When he's on the afterdeck, the *Pertinax* looks like a peacock! They say he sailed into Naples, and crowds turned out—thought he was the pope!"

"When you see him, tell him whatever he wants is all right with me."

"We'll bear that in mind around Boston," Mavryck said.

The ketch returned at the appointed time, and Mavryck returned to Boston with a basket of smoked trouts. And with many a caution from Chuck as to how they should be prepared and served. Rufus Achorn, Mavryck said, would fix them for supper, and Mavryck would have a few friends in for flip and trout. At mention of Rufus, Elzada was minded to send him a note in French. She did, and Mavryck carried it. She asked him to go to Miss Beddington and have her make six dresses— three each for Nora and Chuck. All to Chuck's measurements, but—and then Elzada wondered if Rufus would be able to handle reef points. Knittles? She wrote reef points in English and underlined. It wouldn't be necessary for Rufus to know about reef points—Miss Beddington would. And Miss Beddington did. The dresses arrived in time and fit beautifully. The bill went to Townes Estate.

33

In 1677, as Mavryck foresaw, the Massachusetts Colony came to terms and bought all the rights to the province of Maine from the heirs of Sir Ferdinando Gorges. These rights derived from the charter of 1639, Charles I to Sir Ferdinando, and encompassed what Elzada knew as "to the west'ard." The province of Maine of the Gorges heirs petered out along about the Penobscot, but willy-nilly Elzada's part of the far-down coasted along with Massachusetts.

Having heard nothing of this transaction yet, Elzada and Norman were at Wednesday supper. She said, "I'm writing to Mavryck, and I'm telling him to draw the final papers on our agreement."

"I thought it was after ten years?"

"It doesn't need to run that long. You can leave and I've got to pay you. I can kick you out, and I've got to pay you. What kind of a deal is that? But, what else could we have come up with at the time? I'm happy, and if you're happy—that's it. Shall I send this letter along?"

"Do you want to?"

"Thanks, Norman. That was just the right thing to say. Yes, I do. They way things have worked out, we're not in the same boat we were in the beginning. We had no way to expect the Townes windfall. That shouldn't change anything. So, why not have Mavryck put the shysters to work, and we'll settle everything for good. You'll have a chance to see the papers when you sign them, and meantime, I've made a memorandum to cover you if I drown, or worse. All right?"

"Of course."

The other farm business had been discussed, and the meal was almost over when Norman spoke:

"Elzada?"

"Yes?"

"No—I didn't *say* it. I *asked* it."

"What do you mean?"

"It's not a common name."

"No."

"Elzada. I've been meaning to ask you about it ever since I knew you."

"I imagine I'm the only Elzada. When I was small I supposed it was from the Bible, but I never could find an Elzada in the Bible. I was named for my father's sloop."

"My great-grandmother was named Elzada."

"She *was*!"

"Yes, except she spelled it with an *e* instead of an *a*—Elzade."

"In French it would be Elzade instead of Elzada—Marie-Paule Marcoux always called me Elzade—*el-zahd*."

"My great-grandmother *was* French. Her son was Jabez, my grandfather, the boatwright."

"Interesting—my father's name was Jabez."

"Well, this Jabez, my Jabez, taught us to make boats, all of us—his sons, and their sons. We never did time at the trade—always a family tradition. Jabez was a master builder. Might say he was the first of the family . . ."

"First?"

"Well, yes—you see, he changed the name. Old French name was Kwintail, way they said it, and he didn't like that so he changed it. Ever since, we've been Kincaids."

"Which is a very fine name," said Elzada.

"I suppose—but that was a long time ago and it doesn't matter now."

CREDITS, SOURCES, AND
ACKNOWLEDGMENTS

William Pendleton, Searsport, Maine
Samuel Pepys, London, England
Winthrop's *Journal*
Williamson, *History of Maine*
Abbott, *History of Maine*
De Mont's Voyages, Mark l'Escarbot
Massachusetts Historical Collections
New York Historical Collections, Boston Athenaeum
Local histories—Portsmouth, Berwick, Scarborough, etc.
The Length and Breadth of Maine, Stanley B. Attwood
A Brief Narration, etc., Sir Ferdinando Gorges
History of Brunswick, Wheeler
*Les Singularités de la France Antarctique, autrement
    nommé Amérique*, André Thêveî
Jesuit Relations
James Rosier
Trending into Maine, Kenneth Roberts
Ancient Dominions of Maine
Biard's Relation
Hazard's Historical Collection (Lady de Guercheville)
Le Saint-Laurent et ses Îles, Damase Potvin (Quebec, 1945)
L'Île d'Orléan, Quebec, 1928
Howard I. Chapelle
Maritime History of Maine, William Hutchinson Rowe
Memorial Volume, Popham Celebration, 1862
Public Records Office, London, Chapel of the Rolls
        Charter of James I, Virginia
        Subsequent charters, patents, and grants

Garneau's History of Canada
Netherland Colony petition to the prince of Orange, 1620,
   and subsequent resolutions
Commission to Gorges by the king, July 1637
Kennebec Grant to William Bradford
Jocylyn's Voyage to New England
York County Archives, Lillian W. Gould and Minna
   Thompson
Areopagitica, John Milton
Breda Declaration of Intent, Charles II
Colonial Living, Edwin Tunis
Shirley Grunert Martin, University of Maine at
   Farmington